Depending on the Light

Thea Hillman

Manic D Press
San Francisco

To my teachers in grade school and high school,
Ms. Shipounoff, Katy Hutchins, Ms. Phillips, Mrs. Courtois. For noticing.
And to you.

Appreciation and apologies first and foremost to the victims of my fiction. Thanks to all of my family for showing up and being proud even when I'm reading about sex. Thanks to those who made creating a book feel so wonderful and so necessary: Storm Florez, Diane Fraser, Emily Galpern, Daphne Gottlieb, Victoria Heilweil, Ginu Kamani, Melissa Kaye, Janet Kincaid, Kate Lambert, Kendra Lubalin, Michelle Matz, Lael Robertson, Cynthia Scheinberg, Elizabeth Stark, and Elizabeth Willis. Thanks to Bo Bogatin. Thanks to Steve Fried of Lunar Offensive Press for being my first publisher and friend. For always modelling fabulousness, Carol Queen and Robert Lawrence. For her calm in a moment of crisis, Kim Webb. Thanks to the boys of Market Street Kinko's and to everyone at Pier 9. Thanks to those who opened their ears, hearts, and homes on the road. For elevating book covers to high fashion and making a dream come true, Rex Ray. For making another dream come true, and for her strength and vision, Jen Joseph.

Grateful acknowledgment is made to the following publications, recordings, and websites in which some of these writings appeared in slightly different forms: *Beaten to the Bone, Berkeley Fiction Review, Bull Horn, Comet, First Person Sexual,* GettingIt.com, *Libido,* Lunar Offensive Press, *Mouth: Best of the San Francisco Word Scene, On Our Backs, Queer View Mirror 2, San Francisco Bay Guardian.*

Cover design: Rex Ray

Library of Congress Cataloging-in-Publication Data

Hillman, Thea, 1971–
  Depending on the light / Thea Hillman.
    p. cm.
  ISBN 0-916397-70-X (pbk. : alk. paper)
  1. Lesbians--Literary collections. I. Title.
PS3608.I45 D46 2001
810.8'09206643--dc21

                                                2001001601

Distributed by Publishers Group West

Language often looks like a riot or an orgy.
                                                —M. M. Bakhtin

CONTENTS

I

She came like haiku
Five (breath) seven five (breath breath)
Trembling air then gone

States of Undress

We're driving through them, the states of undress unwinding like letters, a dear, a love, a confession. Un. The undoing of the country. Crossing lines, one by one by one, buttons, through holes, eased by gasoline and lipliner. Slipping across the states, humid, hot, and open. Gaping states, receiving women like rock stars, like relatives, like refugees. Receiving poets like women, like comrades, like visitors with alien plates. The further we go, the more we take off. Dropping garments like r's, like s's, the hotter it gets, the more walls fall, the more I become we, the spaces between the seats gets smaller, sweat has no origin, clothes soaked, as in undress, plastered. At night. In yet one more bar.

Erotakill

I drive
I drive
I drive
Pressing you
Pushing you
Press
You
Over
And over
And over
Until you
Become one
With the pavement

Holding Pattern

Panel, high-low, floor, mix, defrost. Panel, high-low, floor, mix, defrost. Maybe if I keep reading the climate control dials on the dashboard, I won't feel the arm between my legs that isn't your arm. If I stare straight ahead, panel, high-low, floor, mix, defrost, they won't see I'm clenching my teeth and that my eyes are red-rimmed. If I hold still enough, maybe I won't feel the gearshift I'm straddling, squished between these two women, this gearshift that outvibrates my Hitachi magic wand, maybe I won't wince at the arm that hits my breast every time she shifts. In this dyke truck from hell, she says, "I don't sell it because I live in the Mission." All dykes have the same excuse for keeping old trucks no matter what neighborhood they live in. Why can't they just admit that paint-peeling, rust-scraping, smog-causing trucks make them feel like shit-kicking bad asses?

Maybe if I keep holding it in, my hand braced against the dash because there are no seatbelts and that's the only thing that'll save me in an accident anyway, panel, high-low, floor, mix, defrost, excuse-me accidental touches and jokes about road signs and now beginning the scenic route won't seem so heartbreaking. Because all of this, all of this, makes not having you even harder. And maybe, if I don't say anything, maybe if I keep my mouth shut tight, they won't hear me rage against their half-thawed TV-dinner conversation. They won't hear me mourn beige arrangements and Tang-tinged negotiations, won't hear me scream for anything that bites through my steel, slaps me silly, and sings as hard as I do. And they won't hear me cry out for you.

If I hold still enough, the sides of my head a vice to keep the terrifying living things in, really it isn't them at all, panel, high-low, floor, mix, defrost, really it's you who broke my bland, stable platonica, you who stuck your fingers in but only so far, you who wants to be a fly on my wall but not in my bed, you who breaks down all my walls, leaving me with the ruins of tough girl when I don't come as you fuck me, saying girl who looks out, saying look at me but don't see me, asking what it felt like when I thought I'd never see you again, you who left a bruise the size of a hoof print on the inside of my thigh. You, fuck you for making my pulse quicken at the scent of cigarette smoke. Fuck you for being a writer. Fuck you for being an amazing writer. Fuck you for being someone everyone knows. Fuck you for being in a screwed-up, non-monogamous relationship that got you this close to me and this far from me. Fuck you for moving the boulder that I didn't even know was holding everything in. Fuck you for showing me I was full to bursting when I thought everything was well contained. And fuck you for sticking your fingers in. Fuck you for sticking your fingers in. Panel, high-low, floor, mix, defrost. Fuck you for sticking your fingers in. And fuck you for pulling them out.

Having Holly

It was so hot. Can I just say it was the hottest sex I've ever had with a woman—practically fully clothed the entire time? As good as the best boy sex I've ever had. Except it was Holly.

Maybe it started when I could crack sexual innuendos, and she fired them right back; She was nasty too. Or showing up at her birthday. We were the only women wearing flowing skirts in a room full of argyle and crew necks. Or her room. The pillows on her bed—flushed peach and blue, red—pastel, but not shallow, light. Embracing. A flash of me holding Holly on that bed was how I realized I was attracted to women. And more specifically, Holly.

So is she going to call or what?

Years of moving around ensue, but somehow we stay close. I come out to her via airmail. She writes back she is, too. She flirts with me over the phone. Goes to a wedding nearby and is too busy to call. She's scared, I think.

I mean, it wouldn't be so weird if we hadn't gotten together.

Another year goes by. Then we see each other. I've changed a lot. She's intimidated. I think, good, I'm not attracted to her anymore. I go to dinner to meet her mom, her aunt, her grandparents. And it's all so innocent that we drink wine and I make her family laugh and they like me and I'm sleeping over.

If only she didn't stroke me afterward, caressing me with so much tenderness.

After dinner, lying in her high school pink ruffled bed, teenage girls at a sleepover, I wonder why we keep returning to the subject of sex. And why when her lover calls and she breaks their date, she lets him wonder what's going to happen that night.

I tell her I'd rather have my hair played with than be fucked.

Cuddling, friends, "non-sexual" of course. She holds me. It's nicer than I ever could have imagined to be held by Holly. She jokes about how beautiful our children would be. My head against her breast. Her fingers in my hair.

Neither of us is taking responsibility.

Excruciatingly, strokes lengthen. Fingers stray close to sensitive ears. Fingers splay open over faces. Hands slip under t-shirts. Hair is tugged. Strokes are held—hesitating—then deepening. Strong hands are complimented. Little moans escape. Bigger moans escape. Bodies shift. And it's not so suddenly that I realize sex is happening with Holly. And the girls who usually have so much to say to each other are silent.

I don't want to be sexual with Holly unless I can knock her socks off.

Years of wanting, denying wanting, unconscious jealousy, and fear fill my fingers as they love Holly. The same love that's always been there, open, that's no longer being mentioned, that's completely different now, or might be.

We scratch, using nails through scalps, down necks.

I can't seem to do anything wrong. Holly moves with every touch, and all I want to do is keep her moaning with my "non-sexual" stokes. Her head is tilted back, mouth open. I'm too scared to make a sound; she might stop running her fingers through my hair, might stop getting closer and closer to my breasts as she rubs my back. The only thing I'm thinking is come on, bitch, stick your fingers in my cunt, bitch, touch my breast. Over and over, until she finally does make a move. I tighten my legs around hers and let my fingers dig in.

We don't kiss. That would make it real.

We grind. Rubbing through underwear, boxers. Rip t-shirts off. Don't talk. Grab asscheeks. Bite, hard. Scratch. Sweat so hard we slide against each other as we clutch and push our bodies as close as they can get. I want her so badly; I enjoy sliding fingers along her asshole. All I want is to make her come. For her to see how hot we are.

She's told me she loves me, but she's never called me amazing before.

And she's close to coming. And we stop. Holding each other, stray hairs clinging to our sweat, we laugh. She speaks first, whether you like it or not, you're soft and sweet.

I call first. She says she's happy it happened. She'll call me later on in the week.

Phrases fill my head like you know I'm not expecting anything. I know Holly's track record with women, and it scares me. But she's glowing and stroking me with so much care that I decide to expect the best from her. I'm just not sure what that is, and I worry because it's clear to me that I could fall in love with Holly.

She still hasn't called.

And I call her. She isn't stressed or upset. I take this as a bad sign. I cook dinner. She makes sure I know she put on lipstick after she got off BART, on her way to my apartment. She brings me flowers and asks me when I grew breasts.

Holly, what is it about you that makes me write?

I think of calling her in New York sometimes. Urgent. Because she might get married at any time. Because I need to tell her how much I love her. Because I am in love with her.

Writing Holly is having Holly.

But I don't. And I can't seem to write to her. So I use her name. Write her. Because in writing Holly I am loving Holly.

Again and again.

Jesse's Girl

I fucked your girlfriend last night. I reached into you by reaching into your girl. It was a terrible power I had last night. Cold and hard, knowing and not telling, itching with the explosive closeness of it. I fucked her to pieces. Now in between the pieces of her are pieces of shrapnel me, little sharp details of me. I fucked myself into her, indelibly, unsuspecting carrier that she is, so that even as you try to forget me, your girlfriend will remind you.

You and your secrecy made it so easy. Of course she had no idea who I was, flirting with me at the bar last night. She has the sweetest way of flirting, doesn't she? The way she raises her left eyebrow and then lowers her eyes? Sexy and unsure at the same time? How long has it been since she looked at you that way? She was so easy. So hungry. She told me all about you. She told me her girlfriend was a mess and that you'd never talk to her about anything. I feigned protective indignation and told her she deserves better. And she told me she needs to fuck more people like me.

You left these gaping holes in her, holes I know only too well. Fucking her, knowing that, I was fucking myself. I fucked her with all the anger I never gave you and while I think she got more than she bargained for, she never said no, stop, or nothing. Just took it all, moaning and tears streaming. She was right there, eating up my anger at you because she recognized it. She looked her anger in the face and said come fuck me.

And in the evilness of it all, maybe I was you, listening to her stories, taking her like I did, my hand creeping to her throat. You know I wished her dead sometimes, when she was just the girlfriend, the so-called reason we couldn't be together, my hand crawling up between her breasts, pinning her down by her throat, her whole body from the neck down pushing up off my bed, my grip strangling her as she came. After, she said she hadn't been fucked so well in a long time. She said she'd never been strangled before. Funny, since that was the first thing you ever did to me, my head hanging off the edge of the hotel bed, choking, dying inside already because I knew I'd never have you. Why didn't you ever do that to her, Jesse? What didn't you let loose? What were you trying to hold in? Or maybe you wanted to kill something in me? Snuffing out that moment of ignition, recognition even as you fanned it?

I'm sending you a human letter bomb. What's she going to take back to you? If she shocks you by slapping you one of these nights, just know that's from me. When will it dawn on you, I wonder. What little ignorant detail will unwind the string that's wrapped so tight the flesh has turned angry white above and below? You've tied knots so tight. What will your face look like as they unravel? You, as always, will say nothing, holding everything in; yours is the silence of secrets. What will she take back to you from me? Maybe the lesson you taught me, that in moments of fatal errors, accidents, tumors and murders, we give everything up. Confusion clears, passion becomes, precious appears, and we see all that we cannot have.

Passion's Address

Pick a line anywhere and sex
the white dotted line on the blueprint that's my body and sex
the line from hand to outstretched hand
the line from wrist to ankle head to heart throat to groin sternum to
    ass
pick a line and flay me
dissect me at any point and you will find passion and sex
little green passions that ride teaching buses learn about homelessness
    and how to get along and sex
yellow tractor passions digging and lifting the huge metal covers from
    the heartfelt asphalt holes and sex
there is sparkle passion of dark eyeliner lipstick and sex and sex
the pewter pine basket passion washes lemongrass eyes takes walks in
    every kind of weather and sex
puzzle passion looks hard a thousand iridescent scales breathes heat
    and doesn't want answers or sex
sometimes my passion hibernates because its doors are locked and
    sex
it sleeps until its steam melts seals its breath travels through keyholes
    its rage escapes the confines of control and sex
my passion is my ruler both measurement of degrees lived and the
    direction of my steps and sex
passion rushes the rush of blood the curl of my tongue and sex
passion's arms surround others when it strokes me and sex
passion is the deceptive path to quietness and sex
passion reads me bedtime stories I have authored whispering good
    night me good night me good night me and sex
passion holds the pen sometimes hostage sometimes flinging Jackson
    Pollack thoughts at a napkin scrap edge and sex
passion stretches and arabesques my mind follows but the struggle to
    keep up with is the reason that it never will and sex
passion's address feet cunt mouth hands and sex
come visit and sex
the door is always open and burning and sex

Starfucking Closer to Home *or*
What Happens When You Reach for the Stars and They Reach Back

Anybody can lust for Madonna or Keanu Reeves. I like a challenge with a more realistic payoff. I like grunge glamour, the local girls, the stars that shine out of grubby neighborhood bars. The one who stands in the shadows, smoking, who everybody knows, who knows everybody, who has fucked everyone. The musician, the writer, the artist, the activist, the one who everyone sees around on their bike, goes to see them read, recognizes their truck. The one whose name becomes the name, a syllable, even it's something common, like Anne, because everyone knows which Anne you're talking about. If it wasn't her, there'd be qualifiers like "Little Anne" or "Anne who works at Harvest." The one with her name on fliers and bathroom walls. A name that draws crowds and raises eyebrows. And I don't even have to know any of this about her yet; I can tell it all by the way she stands.

The thing about fucking stars is it's a victory of sorts. Show up with a star and all of a sudden people who have met you nine times will remember your name. But you have to fuck them. Hanging around with them isn't enough. Being their friend isn't enough. You have to have gotten lost in their kiss, made them groan, gotten your fist in, watched their star face contort and strain from the orgasm you've given them. You have to do all this and know that you're getting what others want, and that by association, you're a little bit hotter and a little bit more powerful yourself. Sometimes you can even pass for a star, but deep inside you know you're not.

There are certain rules to abide by when you are fucking a star. First of all, only one of you can be a star. Two-star relationships are tricky. It's unhealthy, dare I say toxic, to have that much ego in one room. It's also confusing. Who wears the hanky and in which pocket? If I wear a hanky to your band's show, do you wear one to my reading? Which brings up interesting philosophical questions: once you are a star, are you always a star? What if you're only a star in certain contexts? What about being a star just because you look like one? If no one recognizes you, are you a star?

Which brings me to my next point about stars. Looks are everything. Clothes are lifeblood. Grunge Star musts: a Rock for Choice t-shirt, leather pants, very large boots, latex anything. Hair is a very important part of the star statement, as well. It must be fucked with beyond all recognition. Acceptable product for starhair include: 1. Bleach 2. Wax 3. Acrylic paint 4. Lube. Conditioner is a definite no-no.

Stars are freaks. The first person I ever fisted was a boy who shared his poppers and his animal porn. Then there was the star who squirted so far when I fucked her that she basically watered her plants from across the room. Or the one who suffocated me and called me bitch and told me she was going to kill me. Or the one who sat on the ledge of her tub, when I was in it, pissing on me and bringing handfuls of piss to her mouth to drink, telling me lots of people do it.

And then there was fucking a whole band. I won a date with the band Frat Boy 51 by being on a dyke dating game. We were given $25 for the date which was supposed to cover dinner or rollerskating, or whatever else, depending on how the night went. Two members of the band were friendly and pleasant on the date, but L, the only single one, was solely concerned with how we were all going to get fed on $25. We used the money for safe sex supplies. I consoled L by buying her a burrito.

I am constantly amazed by how insidious dyke stardom is. The best was me going to a reading by a locally famous dyke, B. She read this story about an affair she had, lambasting the whole cool-dyke S/M scene. Like a good writer should, she filled her story with lovely specifics of the affair, how the woman had been on the cover of a fetish magazine, how she let her dog fuck her leg, everything from how she smelled to how she fucked—everything except the girl's name. She didn't have to identify her; all the dykes in the audience were laughing in recognition and I got this creepy feeling that B was writing about the very person I happened to be dating just then, Q. In B's story the woman is really into knives and says, "I won't hurt you, I just want to scare you." And that's when I knew: Q had just used the exact same line on me a week earlier.

Strangely enough, some of the most enjoyable starfucking is finding out after the deed that the person lying next to you is a star. You get all the benefits with none of the annoying social-climber hangover. I call this phenomenon Blind Starfucking. Unlike traditional starfucking where usually the longer you fuck them, the less you like them, in blind starfucking, the longer you fuck them the more starstruck you become. Thus, blind starfucking is a high-risk activity that poses a very real threat to the serious starfucker—there is the potential to fall in love. In fact, I recently succumbed to a disabling bout of blind starfucking that has effectively ended my starfucking career.

I was at the end of month-long spoken word tour across the U.S. My travelling partner and I were thrilled to be performing at the quintessential dyke dive bar in the Lower East Side. One could even say that, for a minute, I was a star. Of course, I spotted her immediately: the lanky blonde with fucked-up hair and a ripped t-shirt, slouching in the corner. Only on the way to her apartment and then in the following months, did I come to find out that she was the publisher of a fabulous underground zine. Then I found out she was friends with three of my favorite performance artists, that she knew my favorite poet, and that her name appeared in two of my most beloved books. Each new aspect of her glittery stardom rocked the foundations of my love-em-and-leave-em starfucker world. But then again, I shouldn't have been surprised. I could have guessed it all from way she stands.

Bad Sex

Telling you about bad sex. Bad sex uplift. Looking back on the moment I knew it'll never get worse than this. Give it to me, your worst bad moment. I want to stroke it hold it cradle it. Because it'll never get worse than this, I promise. It'll never get worse than this. And it won't. For a while. Till the next one. I promise.

Worst bad boy sex, here it is. Jonathan's leaving for good, ignoring the fact that we fucked. And I still have the bruise where he grabbed me when he came. This is when I didn't know that the bruises always last longer. And I'm wearing a shirt that shows the bruise just in case he needs reminding. We're going out, a whole group of us, to say good-bye. And I'm drunk. And it wasn't even good sex. He never knew that I never came. So I'm drunk. Climbing the scaffolding on St. John's Cathedral. Climbing as if to escape this bad sex city. Clinging to no one in that bad sex city, but the scaffolding, ten twenty forty fifty feet, losing the others, losing the buttons off my shirt, climbing higher, like I really wouldn't mind falling, as long as it's extreme and away from here.

I arrive home at four a.m. Dan, the 19-year-old upstairs, is having a party and he wants to fuck me, stupid boy. I tell him, get me off first, then I'll fuck you. He wants to know how I know his shlong won't get me off. I tell him I know, I just know. Maybe it has to do with the fact that the Olympics make him feel patriotic and periods make him sick. Bad bad bad bad sex. So he does get me off, then he's fucking me. Fucking me silently, furiously, frustratedly. And stupid stupid stupid me asks him, what can I do for you? And he says shut the fuck up, you talk too much. And I say get the fuck out. And he says you're so fucking weird and can I have some orange juice before I go? And I know, I just know. It's six a.m., my hangover is looming, I just know. It'll it'll it'll never get worse than this. Bad bad bad. These are the times that try. These are the times that try. These, these are the times that try men's.

Bad sex is the stuff you buy on the street, man. You got a funny feeling but you buy it anyway. Bad feeling bad move bad sex. And you start thinking, there's funny shit in that bag, man, there's funny shit in that bag. But you buy it anyway. Because you're desperate, you need it, and it goes down hard. Comes out bitter bad bad leaves a bad taste in your mouth. And after, you tell yourself, no one needs it that bad. No one needs anything that bad. No one needs anyone that bad.

Bad bad bad bad sex. Lick the underside of my arm bad sex. Lick my armpit and taste acrid alkaline it's so bad you can taste it bad sex. I want you to taste it, leave you with a bad taste in your mouth, taste it, chewing on tinfoil, taste it, feel it, flossing with my tampon string bad sex.

Bad sex in retrospect. Often worse looking back bad sex, when I didn't even realize while I was having it how bad it was bad sex. Digging my fingers in your thigh as I cum, you say no Thea no Thea no Thea. And I hiss yes yes yes. I like being told no. I want to hurt you, want to bite right through your neck bad sex. Shoot my fingers through the skin of your thigh through the cage of your body my lip folded back against my face by your chest. Yes. I want to hurt you when I cum. I look over when it's over and you're gone. You're just gone gone gone. You're at her house in your head, thinking of her, damn you. You tell me I'm smart from seven miles away, I say tell it to my face my face my face.

I'd fuck an accent if I could. That's all I want. Accent essence sans reticence sin body. Dump the body, baby. And you say no Thea no Thea. And I say yes. Dump the body. And I say yes.

Found in the Envelope Taped on the Front of My Desk in Third Grade
on Valentine's Day

Valentine to the Writer Who Lives Alone
So when we get to my house, Karen asks if she can use the
bathroom, which is as good a way as any to get inside my apartment.
And when I hear the flush, I think, damn, did I flush after that last
shit? Because sometimes I don't flush when the cats are in there lying
down or playing because it scares them or if I've been on the phone
I don't flush because I don't want to draw attention to the fact that
I've been multitasking. After Karen leaves I go in to the bathroom
and notice I've left busride poem scrawls on the windowsill, right
where someone could see them as they washed their hands. I realize
I'd rather someone see my shit than my raw poetry.

*Valentine to the Three Young Girls Walking Ahead of Me on Market Street
Towards the Castro*
I have them pegged: they're eighth graders, walking close because
they need the security of the pack, longish lanky hair because they
need the curtain for protection, tennis shoes and baggy jeans because
they need the androgynous security to hide the halfway breasts and
maybe hips. And as I'm thinking all this I see the one in all black has
a pink triangle pin on her backpack and I look closer and see the
gay/lesbian/bisexual center pin right next to it. And I think, this
eighth grader knows way more about herself than I do.

A Valentine to the First Boy I Ever French Kissed
I remember telling my first boyfriend, Noah Blackwell, that I
loved him, even though I wasn't sure if I did or if he loved me back.
Those words were so powerful I didn't know if something would
happen if I used them when it wasn't true love, like a curse or some
bad magic thing. I still don't like to write the words I love you on
paper. What happens when you break up? I am so scared for those
words to lose meaning, for them to be glassy, empty evidence of my
vulnerability.

Valentine to a Crush

She asks me if she can pee on me and I say yes, as long as she keeps me warm. Then we fall asleep holding each other, which God and all of my ex lovers know is a rare occcurence and I wake up in the middle of the night with my hand on her pussy and I panic that I have fallen asleep while getting her off and I ask her, real cool-like, "Is there something I'm supposed to be doing?" and wake her up by asking, so I must not have been fucking her. She can wreak like one of Miriam's 18-clove garlic sandwiches or like something rotten or mildew. She scratches at her hair like she's trying to shake something out of it and yet I can't get over the taste of her first thing in the morning and I want to kiss her for hours and this could sound like love or an awful big crush, but it's not because we're not even dating.

Valentine to this Girl I Used to Go Out With

When she talked about old girlfriends she'd always say, "This girl I used to go out with," and I thought she didn't want me to know their names, that she was keeping things from me. Then I mentioned one of her exes by name and she cringed. I think she didn't want hear their names aloud; she wasn't keeping them from me, she was keeping them from herself.

Valentine to Singles

The addict tells me she can't get too close to me because her addictive personality will make her have expectations. We are all addicts. Whatever natural urge we had to mate, merge, et cetera has been amplified a million-fold by outside pressures that tell us we aren't okay alone, that we aren't whole unless we have a better half. Are we simply a bunch of halves walking around? The halves and the halve-nots? Are halves just wandering around waiting to be wholed?

Valentine from My Inner Necrophiliac

I'm making you a valentine. The half-moons of your fingernails make a lovely scalloped edge, like french manicure lace. The hair from your head weaves cursive, with pubic curlicues flying off where customarily the pen leaves the page. The delicate thigh-skin parchment has crisped and yellowed without its connection to the body, blood, and cells that fed it and kept it wet, pliable.

Let me count the ways, the infinite art projects that are you. You become a valentine to yourself, from me to you. Touching you inside, opened up, makes me want to fingerpaint. I understand you this way. Cutting smaller shapes from the whole. In school, I always loved the negative space, the edges left over from what was cut. Made my valentines from the outlines, from what others threw away.

My hands are red-soaked, made clotted and clumsy with you, and your valentine looks a little sloppy, like a child made it, after the years when the teachers made the kids' artwork and before the kid had any coordination or taste but was given access to household art supplies: dried noodles, doilies, glue, and candy hearts.

But it suffices, my valentine captures your essence.

Valentine to the Hopeless Part I
What's the difference between love and herpes?
Herpes is forever.

Valentine to the Hopeless Part II
This is what I know about love. In fifth and sixth grade I have the same teacher, Mrs. Martin. In the second year, I ask her how love can last, because I have no idea and she's been married for seven years and she's still in love with her husband. I remember her thinking about it and getting back to me the next day. Telling me about love and how she still gets excited to see him and I remember being relieved, but doubtful.

Love was my parents fighting, a lot and loudly. Me telling my brother we had to be good or else they'd get a divorce. I asked them if they were going to get a divorce and they said no, that adults just argue sometimes and that it's normal, so I figured then that it was all in my head and that to live with two adults who disagreed on everything from parenting to keeping the windows open or closed must be normal. And I decided if this was normal, I wanted no part of it.

When I was in high school, my parents finally admitted they were thinking of separating. I had this strange 'I told you so' feeling, knowing that what I'd grown up with wasn't okay or what every kid is supposed to grow up wanting. Sometime while I was in college, my parents raised the white flags of compromise and they are staying together. And it's true that my mother travels to Nepal for four months out of every year, but at this point, I say, whatever works.

Valentine to the Next Person I Fall in Love With

I want to write of your beauty and wonder, but all I can think of is fear. I'm afraid of my desire. What if you won't play four-square with me? What if you bounce a tall-trees after a busstop and bounce me out while I'm still in the D-square? What if I come home from camp and you forget to pick me up and I keep looking for your face, keep waiting to be found, to run to you and hug you around your waist? What if we fight all the time? What if we get stuck in patterns in the mud and spin our wheels and need a tow-truck to get us out? What if it's more painful in the end than it ever was wonderful?

Valentine for People Falling in Love

Love is for people who don't know each other. Love is the person I hope can reflect all my craziness, perversion, and hot creation. Love is something I pin on someone, not dissimilar to pin the tail on the donkey, hoping I come somewhat close to the target, but reaching out just the same. And when it's pinned it's pinned and all I can do is watch it run its course.

Love, desire, and need get all confused and they fight and switch clothes just to fuck with me. But all three burn and ache and when mixed are this dangerous chemical compound that releases poisonous gases from my eyes, clouds of readable smoke, inscribed with all my naked wishes and poetry. And these are the times I want to close my eyes to the world, and these are the times they are so wide open I scarcely take the time to blink, usually racing from one club, one bed, to another.

Love is what makes me keep writing and trying and doing it over and over until I get it right.

Amicable

Anne Heche has been hospitalized!
I was walking along to meet Krista for dessert
in the Castro and her dad had died and the baby, maybe Talulah
was due in November and you had broken up with me
and it was warm the way San Francisco nights surprise
when the wind dies down and the air is soft with salt and
night blooming jasmine and suddenly I see a headline
HECHE HOSPITALIZED AFTER BIZARRE INCIDENT
She ran out of gas on Highway 33 wandered in the
heat about a mile along a dirt road to a house on Nebraska Avenue
Aracelli Campiz told reporters, "I was so surprised to see my favorite
actress. She even put on a pair of my slippers."
I had just gotten off the phone with you, telling you
finally, not to contact me and
the deputy wrote in his report: "She proceeded to tell me that she
was God and that she was going to take everyone back to heaven
with her in some sort of spaceship."
there is no snow in Hollywood
there is no breeze in Fresno
They met and got together so fast without knowing
each other
I have been to lots of bars
and acted perfectly disgraceful
but I have never actually been hospitalized
Oh Kate I love you come back

43

If I said it before then probably the breath carried more wait than the words. You tell me not to take her literally but the heart hears before the head hits the paper. Emotions waltz dangerously close to thought's patterns, hopefully repetition is rebirthing without the new age anchor attached. Even if this is true, I can't see you without remembering what we were and how. The kiss is not new unless it tastes of unseen animals and the unspoken. Still I reach for you and call and expect answers from what I already know. Love being what we think we know and no less.

II

Cut me and salt me
Hammer words in my metal
I'm thick-skinned and sweet

Beverly Hills Picnic

Bess walks outside, smelling bacon in the cold L.A. air, watching her reflection ripple on the black mirrored building where her mother is falling asleep artificially. She just witnessed her mother sign a paper that says, "I am aware, that as with any surgery, there is a remote chance that cosmetic surgery may result in disfigurement or death." What, remote as in Nepal?

They arrive, two girls and their moms, at the plastic surgery mini-village, compound, headquarters, at seven a.m. Everything from initial consultation to surgery takes place in this one shiny building. A nurse ushers them into preop. Bess knows her frame of reference is skewed because her first thought is preop, as in transsexuals. As they wait for the doctors to arrive, they search each others' faces: who's getting what done and who thinks what needs to get done on who between the four of them?

Bess is learning that you never know in L.A. People look different in L.A. They put on make-up to go jogging. Maybe it's all the leopard print and fake fur. Everyone wears that stuff in San Francisco, except in L.A., it's the straight people who wear it. Everyone looks altered. There are constant commercials for liposuction and cosmetic surgery for 0% down, especially if you need to lose 75 pounds or more. These are followed by the loan commercials so you can pay for your $20,000 surgery.

The girl is chattering in the preop room next to where Bess and her mom are waiting. In an overly cheerful voice, she tells the nurse she's getting her face done. This girl who is probably 23 is getting her eyes and her nose done. It breaks Bess's heart.

The doctor comes and talks to Bess after he's marked her mom's face, asks her about school and tells her about his work fixing cleft palates in Zimbabwe and Venezuela. Tells her the Masai tribe are beautiful in their own right, but not to him. Calls her "sweetie" and actually is a pretty nice guy. But when her mom comes back from surgery six hours later and she sees what he's done to her, she hates him.

They gave her mom a tranquilizer to help her sleep the night before the surgery, and Bess was like, what about me? She had nightmares all night long. After she leaves her mom at preop, she goes back and sleeps at the hotel and has more nightmares. Someone calls, she panics, runs for the phone, slips and falls, skids on the rug, gets a bruise and rugburn. When Bess answers the phone, she feels so sick to her stomach that she can't even talk.

When her mom gets wheeled back to the hotel by her nurse, she looks so bad Bess can't look into her eyes for fear her mother will see how much Bess hates what she has done to herself. She can't even recognize her. Not a trace of the face she knows. Bess has to focus on her hands to know it's her.

"We're having a Beverly Hills picnic," says her mom's nurse a day after the surgery. A picnic on the third floor of the Beverly Hills Hideaway Inn where people get rolled in in wheelchairs with helmet-sized bandages around their heads and don't leave their rooms for the first four days of their stay, where pus and matted hair and blood on the pillow are as normal as pay-per-view and room service. This is the hotel where the maid tells Bess, "No es hotel, es hospital," and she wants a breast reduction, and she grabs a boob in each hand and pushes them up and down to demonstrate what happens when she runs.

It's during this picnic that her mom says, "This is not the party I had thought it would be," referring to the nausea, insomnia from anaesthesia, constipation from the antibiotics, and not being able to see or eat because her eyes and mouth are so swollen. It is during this picnic that Lori, her mom's nurse and nurse-to-the-stars, tells her that even though Nicole Kidman and Tom Cruise are married, they are both gay. No shit, right? Next, she tells Bess that her daughter goes to the same school as Sidney Simpson and that both being 5'8" in seventh grade, they became fast friends. And unannounced to her, O.J. has been picking up the two girls after basketball practice and taking them for ice cream. Lori tells her that no one, not even Steve and Candice Garvey, no one, thinks O.J. is innocent.

While her mom's with the nurse, Bess escapes and goes to see Cathy Opie and Cindy Sherman's work at the MOCA. Cindy Sherman's close-up, double-page spread of the swollen, crusted half-human, half-monster face is exactly what her mom looks like right now. She has now been sick to her stomach for two days.

And Bess starts getting this strange empathy, like the intense period of mourning she went through for roadkill a while back. Every time she'd see roadkill she'd think about the lost life of the animal and whose pet it was and what cute things it did when company came over, except this time the intense empathy is for things crushed and broken, like crunched-in cars, as if the force of impact and its permanence equals how damaged women are that they'd intentionally inflict all this extreme suffering on themselves in the name of what? And so it's L.A., she's driving all over the place and each dented car hurts.

It's all about mirrors in L.A., mirrored buildings, mirrored shades, tinted windows. It's about impermeable surfaces reflecting you back at yourself. Bess reads her mom a short story called "Mirrors" about a couple that has a summer home without mirrors and how this couple, man and wife, mirror each other. And they're stuck in this hotel room, time-warped, her mom unable to see or open her eyes and then being able to see and checking herself repeatedly in the mirror and Bess holds her breath, tense when her mom does look, hoping she can't see in the mirror what Bess sees, the stitches on her eyes, the stitches that go all the way around her face, under her chin, behind her ears, the bruised, bloody distended face, and Bess hopes most of all the thing that's hardest to hope, that the fact that this is her mother does not mean that she will mirror her and do this same thing to herself one day.

Sticky Yellow Tags

She's not dead, spoke Yiddish fluently. Getting onto the freeway at 25 miles per hour, Alzheimer's or old age or something has struck. She gave me my first dictionary and thesaurus. I was a poet even then. Part of her is dead. Memorize the planets.

I'm talking about her like she's dead because she makes me. She asked each of us to put our names on the things in her house that we want. When I helped her move everything had these sticky yellow tags with members of the family's names on them. But they kept falling off because they were just attached with the adhesive that's on sticky pads and so Grandma stuck them back on whatever she could reach.

She keeps sending me Immodium. In fourth grade my favorite book was the thesaurus. If a boy tells me I have to prove my love to him by having sex I should tell him I don't have to. It's a lady's duty to patch things up. I should invite him to a nice dinner. Am I my grandmother's keeper?

Grandma's new house and everything's off, just tilted, angled into the room, barely not centered. Can't anything, even by mistake, be level? It's a numbers game, couldn't one picture have ended up straight? She's put up and taken down the pictures from her walls so many times that they are riddled with holes. There are gold gilded wooden frames next to metallic gold next to steel black next to iridescent multicolored wooden next to white plastic. I could spend all day adjusting the couch, nudging the table.

Then there's the recent letter. He was all over me. She'd take me to the library, solved the *New York Times* crossword puzzles. Why am I letting her drive? Little strokes that go unnoticed. Translator of German and French, her handwriting slides off the page. I could pick out all the books I wanted. The address is different every time. Sitting on two phone books. The evil curse. A brilliant oversight of the medical profession.

Grandma's constantly amazed at how smart I am because I remember the way out of her apartment complex. She got lost driving to Payless today which is one block away. She told the sales clerk that the calculator and safety pins she'd bought hadn't been in her bag when she arrived home last time. He patiently went over everything that she bought last week and explained that she had decided not to buy the calculator and hadn't bought safety pins, and what's it like? If I exercise every day will that still happen? Is it broccoli? Is it vitamins? Is it dying young?

Sideswiping parked cars. Part of me wants to capture what I remember. Huge line at Sizzler. She's not who she used to be. Because she lied to the hostess. She keeps sending me Immodium. Everything had these sticky yellow tags.

What the Dead Do to the Living

I wonder if she still smokes and I think why not and how it used to be that anyone who smelled stale reminded me of her. Now it happens only once in awhile and I almost miss it, remembering the hesitation I'd feel when I'd lean to kiss her goodnight, holding my breath, and then giving in and breathing anyway because it was her smell.

I couldn't wait to grow into her, those coral nails and pearly Florida toes that peeked from silver sandals decorated with rhinestones, pebbles, shells. I wanted to wear sandals like that someday. I couldn't wait. Maybe that was the problem. We'd go shopping and she'd complain that I picked out the most expensive thing in the store. I just wanted to look glamorous like her, drinking cocktails, watching soaps.

I see her now, from the old picture at the beach where I can see myself in her face. I see her now across an endless golf green where sandpits fall into the ocean, paths paved by playing cards. She's wearing the red bathing suit with the matching scarf, the hi-cut low-cut suit with little laces at the thigh and bodice. One hand on hip, the other tosses back handfuls of mixed nuts. Bubby watches me, laughing, loving me as she never did, loving my high heels and blonde hair. She cheers my tight skirts, erotica, and push-up bras. As the only granddaughter, I was the natural choice to carry on the partygirl gene, but she had her doubts, me such a chubby girl and those braces and those glasses.

I feel her winking. And sometimes feel her jealous fingers at the clasp at the back of my neck, reaching for the diamonds she couldn't take with her.

Lover's Kaddish

Yitgadal veyitkadash shemei raba bealma divera chireutei, veyamlich
It's just the sound it's just the sound it's just the words
Malchutei bechayeichon uveyomeichon uvechayei dechol beit Yisraeil,
I don't know the words I know the sound I know the sound
Baagala uvizeman kariv, veimeru: amein.
I stumble on the words I say the rhythm I say the rhythm
Yehei shemei raba mevarach lealam ulealmei almaya.
the rhythm and the jew and the poet and the jew
Yitbarach veyishtabach, veyitpaar veyitromam veyitnasei, veyithadar ve
the rhythm is the way we rock is the way we pray is the way we fuck
Yitaleh veyithalal shemei dekudesha, berich hu, leeila min kol birechata
is the way we pray
Veshirata, tushbechata venechemata, daamiran bealma, veimeru:
the old woman in the movie asks the camera "who will say the kaddish
    for me?"
amein.
I say the kaddish for her the words in a language I don't know, stumble
    on trans-
Yehei shelama raba min shemeya vechayim aleinu v'al kol Yisraeil, vei
literation, I stumble and say everytime for her the rhythm is for her
    the way I rock is
meru: amein.
for her the words of the prayer I don't know the only prayer I know
    means life
Oseh shalom bimeromav, hu yaaseh shalom aleinu v'al kol Yisrael, vei
affirming I know this in my elbow, I bend
meru: amein.
I know this in my mouth, I ask
I know this in my poem, I call out
I know this in my sleep, I wail
I know this in my fuck, I pray
I know, I bend, I ask, I call, I wail
I sleep, I say, I fuck, I pray, I this

I rhythm, I words, I time, I her, I way
I sound, I poem, I rhythm
I know
the lover's kaddish

Poor Mom/Me

So Bubby died. And I don't have time to sit and write. Except to say that I feel decidedly irritated right now. Damn selfish, I'd say. Death is selfish. Mourning, I mean.

My poor mom. Mom kept saying that and all I could think was my poor mom.

I talked to her a couple of hours after Bubby had died. Mom said she understood if I didn't want to go to the funeral because she knew her mother hadn't been the greatest grandmother, or mother. I felt so bad that she felt she had to say that.

When I was little, I told Bubby I wanted her necklace with the diamonds in it when she died. She used that against me for years. Kind of holding it over my head to taunt me. But she always told me I'd get it.

Both Mom and I feel better in her apartment without her. I feel like I don't have to whisper. I can take a shower, use her towels. She asked me last time I was here, "Why don't you take a shower at the hotel?"

Mom rebelled. She turned all the lights on. Bubby used to say, "We don't have a share in the electric company." We can use the paper towels without feeling guilty. My mom said it was like saying "Fuck you" to her mother.

We broke into the locked cabinet where she used to keep her liquor and smoked salmon. Canadian smoked salmon. We wouldn't've been allowed to eat it. And if we didn't eat the whole can, "Why did you open it then?" If, God forbid, we finished it all, we'd be pigs. I'd need to watch my weight.

She used to watch my weight as carefully as I did. Only two other things, besides being Capricorns, that we had in common: my interest in boys and soaps. She always wanted to hear about my boyfriends. She bet me that I'd be married before I was 21. I always sort of took that as an insult. She watched *The Young and the Restless.*

Poor Mom. She'd talk and her tired eyes would get big and red-rimmed. She didn't really cry. Not in front of me. We drank Courvoisier.

She got drunk. Poor Mom. She'd forget what she was saying. She talked a lot more than she usually does to anyone. She kept repeating one part of the story as she told it. It was the part of the story where her mother dies. She'd say, "Then my mother died." And then again in a few moments, "She died." And then, "I held her hand and helped my mother through her death." She didn't know she kept saying it. I felt really bad for her.

She's been a daughter all her life. Even to my dad. She thinks she'll be stronger without her mom. And now that things between her and Dad are better. She said, her eyes becoming so red again, so sad, that her mom messed her up. Hurt her. Hurt her brother so that he'll never get over it. "Promise me you'll be honest with me. I don't want to mess you up. I don't want to give you what my mom gave me."

My mom listened to Bubby when no one else would. Bubby was so far gone that she could only gurgle and blabber. They pacified her, humored her. My mom listened. Bubby said really beautiful, sweet things to my mom. Things no one would have heard. How frustrating to die and have no one bother to hear the last things you have to say. Mom said, "I love you." Bubby said, "I love you. Just like that, for no reason." Just before she died. She made jokes. My mom said, "Promise me. We need to promise each other to listen. Because they know what they're saying." Mom kept telling Bubby, "I know you're trying to say something. I know it's frustrating; your mind is clear but your mouth won't work." Yesterday, Mom took Bubby outside. Bubby mumbled unintelligibly and Mom said, "Isn't it beautiful outside?" Bubby said, "It's a gift from God. If this is today, what will tomorrow be like?" Mom said, "It'll be a gift from God." Bubby died last night. But only my mom could give her that gift, from God, from her.

How can she make me promise to be that good? That intuitive? I'm so scared I won't be as good for my mom. She says I already am.

A month ago I spilled brisket gravy on Bubby's white chair. "But why did you spill it?" she asked me. There was red, black diarrhea all over Bubby's white chair tonight. Splattered. Ironic. I almost felt triumphant cleaning up tonight. It was like, you may have made me angry and made me feel bad, but I'm stripping your sheets, making your bed for the last time. I'm cleaning up the remnants of you, in your room, your bathroom, even your spots on the kitchen cabinets I'm wiping off.

Mom told me I'm difficult, like Bubby is difficult. I need to "let loose a little" she says. I cried for myself. Bubby is dead and I cried for myself. But I also cry for Mom. Weird. Crying for Mom seems like crying for myself. I feel for her so much that it hurts me. I adore her, I idolize her. All this pain is ending for her. But she's so sad. She has no parents. Crying for her is crying for me.

She looks so angelic sleeping. She looks so happy.

Mom Arrives Home

She carries the Himalayas on her fingers
Nepal in her hair
Her feet that traverse remote mountain passes
Land in this house
With more televisions than humans
In this world but belonging to that

I wonder whose mother you are

Poem to My Mother on the Way to School
When I Had Peanut Butter on My Face

I know why you licked your lips
Just after I kissed you
It was to take the kiss and put it into your heart
I know
I did the same

III

You're not sure if I'm
Butch or femme   I don't wonder
I think that's boring

To Make a Long Story Short

What six words do you use to announce yourself to the world? Do you hyphenate, abbreviate, hesitate, lie? Embellish the obvious, hide the same? Think of little poems, personal ad cardboard panhandler sign, each a poem. Bigger than a bread box, smaller than haiku, *Readers Digest* version of you. Hard thought, deliberately penned.

Certs asks what's the coolest thing your mouth can do? I wanna know. Make the words stand up on the back of my neck. Certs asks what's the coolest thing your mouth can do? If you only have words, Certs says type it with your tongue. If you only have words, even a smile helps. If you only have words, do you lie, guilt, only eight inches or longer need apply? Does god bless turn off more dollars than it? Is homeless vet the best bet? Is well hung and handsome? What makes them give a shit? A call? A quarter? What makes them lean close to drop the change? Act now. Pity. Drop a few coins. There but for. Pick up the phone. Power of words. For the price of a cup of coffee. Holocaust. Fat-free. On sale. HIV. Eviscerating words. Making you taste. Certs is 50 concentrated mints. Split themselves open.

If you only have words, choose your words carefully. Because they can get you fed. Get you off. Get you heard. Get you hard. Get you killed.

Contradiction

I think it was sometime before I was born that wrong crept in. What cell divided when it wasn't supposed to, what tissue held on too long, longing for itself and not giving way? And who told my little brain and what was the energy of difference? Or was it there at all until other bodies defined it so?

This line I walk is somewhere between gardenias and carnations. Sandwiched between blood tests and varsity letters. A charm on the medic alert bracelet. Each visit a tiny X on the line I never was on, weight above, height below. Lines drawn from bone age tests and you have to be this tall before you can ride. If I could have been a hermaphrodite, what does it feel like? No one ever thought to tell me it was okay to feel uncomfortable. Holding difference from the inside out, my appearance as a normal girl is a miracle of medical science. I can successfully reproduce this appearance. I search in others for the parts of me I wronged. My appearance as a girl has crushes on girls who appear to be boys, who are half-boys, who have all the facial hair my mother fought so hard to save me from. The line is about jump rope then. It carries contradictions on its back and I make sure never to step directly on the crack.

My mother says it's rude to contradict. The right answer makes someone else wrong. With contradiction, you can set up wrong any way you want. Contradiction, the epic haiku, the body builder who only likes his feet, opulencia scrawled on Capp Street. You can kick my ass anytime you want, just ask permission first. Contradiction is the circular snake that eats itself, both sides collapsing into the middle, blue and yellow mixed to make a meltdown. It's the guy with permed hair, tennies, and short satin shorts looking for sex on the Castro. It's the tweaker picking garbage off the ground and placing it on car hoods, decorating the dirty decadence of 14th Street. Flesh-colored bandaids. The tiny kitten screaming hallelujah under a landslide of human shit. Ice cream before bed. Things that smell like popcorn. The declawed cat with the spiked collar. Calling and hanging up. The Red Sea and Diet Pepsi. Hating cigarettes but aching for the taste on your lips.

Contradiction can mean speaking against. For me it's about speaking out, about indecision, infinity, oxymorons, ambivalence, being in between, and being everything. Being the freak and passing as normal and being exceptional all at the same time. Contradiction is the bisexual figure of speech, and it's my lifeboat, ferrying me in between genres and genders. Mom says it's rude to contradict. I float above it. I am teaching my mother that my power is my ability to hold contradiction in my arms and then release it, a message in a bottle, rocking on the wide open sea.

Art is Giving Notice

I want to tell you   what my stairs look like striped thin brown
                      orange beige lines three drunken
                      platformed sweaty
                      cigarette-stained flights of two cats
                      the back of San Francisco and women who pay
                      their own rent don't have to be nice

I want to tell you   about this art piece I did a collaboration
                      I don't know the other artist all I did for the
                      piece was notice and name it but maybe
                      that's all art is anyhow so outside Harvest
                      the healthfood store was this charred black
                      circle taking up a whole parking space
                      exploded meltdown of shopping cart metal
                      bright plastic shoe record clothing paper
                      guts spilled burned spewn about in the ash
                      circumference arrested I mourned
                      appropriated took it into myself entitled it
                      House Fire

I want to tell you   my hands are beautiful when wet

I want to tell you   in the moments after we talk
                      I want to sleep
                      or create
                      and anything else
                      is unbearable

Home on the Range

She said do what you're told and no one gets hurt.

I left the knife and spoon and took the fork in the road. When I say road I mean open road and when I say open I mean open. See it's all about home on the range and ranging and breaking homes by leaving them. Breaking and entering, but I don't leave home without it and all clichés work backwards since they were never fit for me.

I left dishes and dates and took a guess.

The fork hung between my breasts. Clanking, tinking, raindrops on a tin roof, tapping a clear path, tapping.

See, I never thought I was a traveler. I have my apartment, my two cats, three houseplants, and occasional long-term lovers, usually without the love but with the long-term and I tell myself I'm a homebody, a Capricorn, bent on creating order and building community and everything in its place and how could I go on the road and leave everything I know?

I left the freak belt buckle, the leather pants, and took five black dresses.

The knife followed us in the form of Swiss army, mace, and many keys.

How could I go on the road, leave my cats and apartment and girlfriend that couldn't live without me? She said you're running. But with running there are times of no foot on the ground. I wasn't running. I was leaving. In the leaving the apartment got spotless, the cats got to eat sugar cereals, and the girlfriend got pissed, got even, and then lived very well, even better, without me. It's all in the leaving, in the leaving home.

I left the umbrella, the flashlight, and took gloves.

So following the triptych and my instinct that said leave at all costs, go no matter what, it'll all work out, I left it all, for a month across the country and back. Slinging poetry in 12 cities, 23 shows, 26 days, 7000 miles. I was sure I didn't want to go out, like Columbus, like Kerouac, and go discover America. I wasn't gonna make these all-knowing, self-important statements about America, always she, right?

America the dream gone bad, America the girl gone bad, America the whore. Instead of making America smaller, encompassing it with pen, mapping it with sentences and confining metaphors, I wanted to make it bigger. I wanted each person to surprise me, to be different than I ever thought they'd be, even though I'd never thought of them before. I wanted to burn new images in my brain and then make that larger too. And my heart. I wanted to see the dots up close, the dots per inch enlarged until they didn't make a face, but rather unmade it. I wanted to not recognize America. Each dot so large and so faceted, so interesting, that America as a concept seemed obsolete.

I didn't miss you while I was away. I was fully gone and you were nowhere near. I didn't miss the cats, my friends, or any material thing. I floated on the road, strings tying me to nothing but the city at hand.

The spoon found me too. Soft and loving hard girls who bent around me.

What I didn't know is that I'd feel at home on the road, that home, as an object, as a feeling, as comfort broke into little pieces, broken glass that reflected me over and over as the light hit me in each different state. Home was the car, Latifah, who Daphne dubbed our summer home. Home on the road was the cooler, filled with nonfat chocolate soymilk, fruit, and makeup. Home was the cooler especially when we stopped for food on the road and all they had was baked potatoes with California veggiess and cheese. These were vegetables that had never been to California and were so processed they tasted like dish soap and the cheese so processed it was watery plastic. Home was finding Sylvia Pojoli, Terry Gross, and Car Talk on NPR between the preaching, country music stations, Covenant trucks that read "It's not a choice, it's a child." Home was having the right outfit at the right time. Home was everyone who was so happy we arrived at wherever we were going, so happy to see us, even though they'd never seen us before. I found I could be myself everywhere I went. I found myself at home wherever I was.

We went flying home, me and Daf, the knife, the fork, the spoon, assorted cups, a variety of dishes, and all the stories we could eat.

I moved while I was away. I would wake in some hotel on the way back, at three a.m. and not recognize the brown light coming in the window. Rock star skin sticks hard: After the trip I would wake every day and wonder how far I had to go, what city I was performing in that night. My world tilted crooked: I would wake and not recognize my own windows and I would wonder who changed the locks while I was gone. I moved while I was away. I am home now. I am readdressing myself.

To Maddie Lou on the Day That You Were Born

Frank, the paper taped to the sidewalk at 9th and Mission panics,
You can win your case if you only show up

There is the mouse chewing tinfoil under the BART tracks
There is the mouse getting blown off the cliff at the beach

Two people in trucks in Nigeria and Tunisia show up and blow up
Obliteration is our international pastime

South Pacific books lean against carefully folded blankets on the
    sidewalk
Maybe I should bring my new neighbors coffee cake or a nice bottle
    of wine

Oh Maddie Lou, I no longer feel better for the country mouse than
    the city mouse
All you have to do is show up and know it's all happening at the same
    time

Doorknocking
for Stuart Matis

They were going door to door on Dolores today. Doorknocking today, on Dolores. My street. Looking shinier and more forthright, or would that be righteous, than anything has the right to look in the Mission. Never seen them on my street before. 22 Fillmore. 16th and Mission, maybe. Tenderloin. Downtown. But do we need to be saved on Dolores?

And the interesting thing is that I have a tremendous amount of empathy for them. Doorknocking is one of the hardest things in the whole world. I did it for 12 hours a day, six days a week, up 14 flights of stairs in eight buildings in the Crown Heights projects, through New York summer and New York winter. I know how tough it is, doorknocking. And believing. Believing is hard. I mean, not believing is hard, but believing is even harder. When you really think you know the answer. Something good. Important. And that it's your job to tell everyone else. And it's your job to get them to change. No, it's your job to save them. A lot of work. Believing. Being right.

Being Mormon. Some of my best friends are Mormon. Really. Always have been, since growing up in a town with a large contingent. Kind and community-oriented and giving. But my Mormon friend Janey, the one who's been in a three-year crisis and depression because she fell in love and had a relationship with a woman. Janey, who could be kicked out of the church, disowned by the only community she's ever known. Janey sent me the email about the tormented 33-year-old Mormon guy who shot himself in front of his church. In California. Because of a lot of things, including Proposition 22. Because he literally couldn't exist in the world as he knew it. And this guy's parents knew he was gay and still loved him. And he still killed himself. Because he believed. What he'd been taught. That he couldn't be Mormon and gay.

I don't believe anymore. I don't doorknock anymore. And maybe violence isn't just explosive moments that we can't take back. Maybe violence roils in our hearts and minds, unformed, and churns like potential in our hands and mouths. And maybe violence isn't black and shiny and hard or sharp. Maybe violence is the fleshy repetition of thoughtlessness, the reiteration of ritual, the written word, and the wisdom of the ages, unquestioned. Knocking. Unheeded. Desire unanswered.

Buckhorn Family Diner

Fifty-five are dead due to the heat wave
There's a waitress about my age, she'd be a dyke if she lived in San
Francisco but this is the Midwest so who knows. Sign at the Country
Kitchen says, *it's different in the country.* And our waitress has got cuts
on her arms, burns? And big green sunglasses hiding a shiner.

And we move right through.
I think about you.
Move through What Cheer, Iowa.
Another Buckhorn Family Diner.
Menu says, *Eat pie! Sweet and salty, wet and dry. There's no taste quite as
fine as pie!*
What is family dining?

There's a tiny abandoned church in Milford, Nebraska. *God is with
you* graces the boarded-up front door. And I'm glad He's with me,
because He sure has forsaken that church.

In Lieu of Flowers
for Matthew Shepard

The pill has gone down the wrong way again
scraping bitter
caught
and no amount of swallowing

I can call Orrin Hatch
I can attend a vigil
I can send money in lieu of flowers
I can go to Laramie
I can email
I can march
I can

Pull the legs off an insect one by one
and ask it to run

Hold my hand over the baby's nose and mouth
now ask it to breathe

Take the skin of the flower in my teeth
pull down the delicate stem
crush it in my palm knowingly
then ask it to grow

I can
I can
I can

I can send money in lieu of flowers
and no amount of swallowing

Equivalence

Light is a knife. Doesn't leave a mark, but its line can be equally stark. Light acts on the body, modifying it, like tattoo, piercing, scar. Light is momentary body manipulation, tells us where we are, belies our crevices, jags, where we are deeply.

My falling for her lasted a year and was sealed by her novel and it was a momentary body manipulation, as just like light it illuminated all that was vibrant and joyful and, like light, when it was gone, it left no trace.

Equivalence: 1: Exchangeability; correspondence. "The Equivalence between the hero's career and that of the author."

Equitability: "The equivalence of mass and energy."

Geologic contemporaneity: "Time equivalency of the Sly Gap to a portion of the Devonian of Iowa is suggested by new paleological evidence."

If you are incalculable, then we are congruent.

Darkness is what gives us shape. Without shade, we are not round. Dark is not the easy way. When you're the doubting Thomas in a room full of nodding nasturtiums, when you're the one who can hold your breath the longest, diving until blue turn to black, when they tell you physics isn't appropriate party talk, you just tell them

1: Density equals mass times volume.
      You just tell them
2: You can't see it's pressing unless you see shadows.

Equivalence: 2: Logic, sameness in truth value. The logical relationship holding between two statements if they are both true or both false.

We hadn't talked for a while. Max and I ran cross country and used to flee the rest of the team, hang out in his dorm room, and listen to Erasure. That's when we were straight. After his boyfriend called and told me the news, I tried to remember the last time we talked. Over two years ago. And then the memories came wandering back. There was the time he came out to me by sending me a letter on the back of a flier for *La Cage aux Folles*. The time we went running together years later in San Diego. The time he kissed me before he moved to Seattle, when his boyfriend wasn't looking. Still, I search for him in crowds of gay men, catching glimpses of him out of the corner of my eye.

Tears from wind and tears from pain are the same.

You want to show me we are the same and I say your blood is not proof. I am only like you in the art of confusion. I don't want blood, I want unrecognizable fluids. I want neither of us to have any idea what is coming out of your body.

Eye: 1. Organ of sight consisting typically of a light-recipient mechanism that regulates the light that reaches a light-sensitive region.

Light passing through the cornea and pupil of the iris is focused by a crystalline lens to form an inverted image of objects in the visual field.

Everything we see is upside down. Our brains then right things, matching objects to things we already know, recognize. Looking for sameness is a trap. In reducing ourselves to comparisons we misdiagnose others. I see you cough and that's how I know I am ill. I see their perfect relationship and that's how I know I am abnormal.

It's a different kind of gaze that really sees. The eye caught by surprise. The moment of perfect detachment. A functioning eyeball detached at the optic nerve from the brain, retina remaining intact.

If you defy definition, then we mean exactly the same thing.

Eye: 5: The direction from which the wind is blowing.

Meditation on Medication

Zovia and Roxane are bitter girls with chemical smiles
Unflowering yellow pink green white in 72-hour release

Roxane rattles her beads against plastic confines
Zovia consults instructions on the blister pack

Persistent sisters they dispense apothecary advice
Anytime you are not sure what to do, do it twice

They say bleeding can lead to looking for sex on Sundays
Studies have found risk subsides with increased breast tenderness

Everyday at the same time I forget them
There is every indication I would miss them if they were gone

Girl Power a la Rimbaud

This is the time of asking questions, the girl who slips in the warm wonderings and bangs her shins on smarting doubts. The one who leaves dangerous potholes in the writhing street. Look, there are things that grow there, and some are hers, picked flowers and matches and clean stories, all erupting new, the finish of one thing that births, or does it, she wonders, another.

Stuffing her dog in her demure purse, she walks on platform heels much too high for her, but the day is here! Thinking like a sage, she quiets the barking and appeases the howl of passion (still zippered), she lines up the shakey words and says dance! and says kick! and says yellow as you are I painted you, so go

Home Alone

Sometimes, I'd rather fuck myself than leave the house.

I center whole days around masturbation. Wake up, eat my cornflakes, clean my apartment, come with my vibrator, vibrator and dildo once, vibrator once again. Fall asleep. Read. Masturbate. Talk on the phone. Masturbate, read, not even wondering if I'm depraved or thinking that it's weird that I haven't gone outside all day, that I came six times today.

It's sweet the way I masturbate when I'm sad. When no one's been as nice to me as they should be. Tears, self-pitying, mix with moans as sharp intake cry-breathing turns into cum-breathing and I start feeling hot and all of a sudden I'm a sexy fucking number, coming hard, forgetting what no one did wrong and remembering how much I get from myself and how much I mean to myself.

I love the sounds I've been hearing lately, that no one taught me how to make—funny, awkward, deep sounds that come from my belly and from my clit. Sounds expressing wonder, fear, anticipation, that sound exactly like me.

I love the stories I'm not afraid to tell. Grabbing my brother's penis under the bath water when I was little, letting my cat lick my pussy. Or watching my guilty flush as I recall playing "I'll show you mine if you show me yours" with my cousin after he showed me the porno movie, *The Budding of Bree*.

I love the questions I'm not afraid to ask. Asking my mother, "How do you masturbate?" And me, dissatisfied with her answer about how people touch themselves and me insisting further, "No, Mom, how do *you* masturbate?"

And the book she got me the very next day suggested looking at yourself in the mirror, so I crab-walked up to the mirror on the back of the bathroom door and that's when I realized it was true—I did have two holes. Which of course I had to explore. And it was kind of tight in there, and that's when I discovered Vaseline.

I love the way I get off on everyday occurrences. Walking down 14th Street, the setting sun like breath on the back of my thighs.

I like watching my late-night posing in front of the mirror, making my cotton underwear sexy by pulling up the corners and lifting my faded olive-green t-shirt just so to showcase my belly curves. Or rubbing my clit while reading *Cold Sassy Tree* to test whether I can come while immersed in rural Georgia in 1906. And I can.

And I still haven't left the house.

Don't Take Her Personally Please

please note she is not responsible for all that she wants or all that she is she is the monkey's middle finger the paper cut she is the shopping cart with the crazy wheel she is the chipped paint of the crosswalk she is the mosquito bite just beginning to scab she is the ink smudge on your fingers that you licked and tried to rub off she is those balls on your sweater under the arms and on the back where your bag hits over and over again as you walk she is the discordant note in a whistle she is the dog without an eye she is the stringy spots on your couch where your cats scratch she is the one regret you can never quite let go of she is the crossed out words that spoke the truth but you were too scared to read them

she does not write incomplete sentences comma every idea she has is embedded in a thousand others and her writing may look logical her clauses independent but truly she wrote them backward and they are a secret code for the oddities that feed her she eats the sexual the offensive gets her up in the morning the world is the way she is different she can promise you you'll disagree she can promise you whatever word you choose she'll infer its second meaning because it's about the spaces and where we place them and where we pause and what we notice

she smells dissent like rare meat she wears the color that isn't she spoons it slowly she takes everything apart especially when she doesn't know how to put it back together she runs on and on because there's no stopping really until we're stopped comma she's too alive to sit by and cry she would if she could but the pulse above her thumb beats so hard she can see the blood dancing under her skin skipping and double stepping her blood is partying her blood is running errands doing the dishes feeding the cat just try and stop her until it runs from her body her blood can't be stopped

she started saving for her death when she was little and now she's on a spending spree because deposits don't accrue they spoil deposits don't accrue they spoil deposits don't accrue they spoil and they never were safe her risks are her battle against complacency and it's so hard not to place the apostrophes she's been well trained well trained well trained well the lessons must end the lessons must end she is the anti-learner the anti-teacher if you learn something from her it's a mistake if you learn something from her it's wrong if you learn something from her it might make you free because she didn't mean to and that's the biggest risk of all for once not to teach not to mean not to do so she's not doing anything and she will not end this with a fucking period

Finding the Girl

This is hide and seek
   little red riding hood and every tale
      where the girl disappears

   she got left at the airport
      lost in the grocery store
         locked in the basement
            left for dead

   she was kidnapped
         neglected
            hit

   her stepmother hated her
      her stepfather abused her
         her mother gave her
away

These are different girls
These are different girls with similar stories
These are different girls with similar stories that always end the same
way
         the girl disappears

She escaped
   ran away
      rebelled
         recovered
            remembered
Now she's my girlfriend and I have to find
         the girl

I find her asleep on the bathroom floor

Behind trees
Playing Nintendo
Fostering sick kittens

I find her despite
Three phone numbers
Two pagers
Broken locks

I find her in a stolen car
Towed motorcycle
Torched truck

I find her between dust motes
Crack houses
Two horses

Now she's my girlfriend and I have to find her

I find the girl by following
                    her need like
        breadcrumbs
                the states on the map
                the lines on the road
                the green exit sign above the door

Now she's my girlfriend and I have to find her

Nobody else bothers

But I find the girl

I find the girl
It takes time
                can opener wrenches slowly
            duct tape introduced to itself
                    rough hands

a crack in the paisley wall
her t–shirt may never come off

I find the girl by remembering her waist
                              hands
                              neck

I find the girl by remembering she's a girl
I find the girl
And then I make love to her like a man
And then I make love to her like a woman
And then I crawl in and play jacks with the girl
                              We tell stories and hold hands
                              but her hand is a faulty night light
                              that flickers and then
                              disappears

Exile
for refugees

    I see this alphabet of sorrow before me and I can barely get my head around the letters and the endless possibilities of arrangement. It's as if every word were a hurt and every sentence a way to explain it. How do I contain human suffering? Is it between two fingers or two people? Is it the two women of different colors at the Castro Home for the Aged passing a pint of Haagen Dazs between them, reaching across the ficus? Is it the bus ride through the Mission? The hunched white man doubled over on the sidewalk? The only time I've ever been scared, a block from my house? Is it the sticker that asks, Do you know your neighbor? And my neighbors who put out their wares on sidewalks that I buy for a dollar and sell back to them next spring? Or my neighbors who put out their wares and their lives along the sidewalk, stolen and gathered possessions that make cement home sweet home? The young Safeway employee riding around on the old guy's electric wheelchair as he stands unsteadily, cheering her on? Is it between the sorrow and the word? Is it the moment suffering becomes art? Is it the moment nothing at all comes from suffering?

    We read and read and read and make noise and make decisions and we're walking fast and we're walking away and we're walking toward whatever meaning is that day and it keeps moving and it keeps shifting. And today I am a Jew and I'm that girl in the resistance and I'm skiing and I'm surviving and I'm betrayed and I'm in the camps. And that fear is mine and I know and I know and I know and that fear means I don't eat or I keep running or I don't spend or I don't trust and then yesterday I was white and I was walking and I was going to school and the school hadn't been shut down and I was passing and I wasn't scared and then yesterday I was a girl and I was chased and I wanted to escape into dark spaces. I wanted the run of the park. I wanted the bushes the bathrooms the seedy inner city I live in but isn't mine. I wanted it and couldn't. And now I am fingers and electric impulses and something goes between me and the computer and I think I'm a body but I'm really a pulsing machine.

I'm really an O or an I. I'm really on or really off and I'm running and I'm working, a good machine, a well-oiled machine, a talking feeling running machine and I pay my toll and I pay for parking and I pay for information and so I pass and I pass and I pass and at the end of the day I'm a receptacle and at the end of the day I eliminate and at the end of the day I secrete and at the end of the day I hold hands and at the end of the day I am warm and at the end of the day I warm another machine and we keep each other warm and we keep running.

Christmas Sucks

I tried to write about sex and Christmas.
I tried to think of jokes about Christmas.
I have this to say: Christmas is not funny.

Scrawled, soggy, wet and left on the sidewalk is a cardboard panhandler sign. It reads, *My boy is seven. Please don't spit on us. Please help us. Merry X-Mas.* The sign is discarded, as if even the panhandler didn't believe the words and tossed it to the ground.

My battle with Christmas started in first grade. Mrs. Haley was making us do dictation with those fat red pencils and aqua-lined newsprint. What do they train us for that we take dictation in first grade? And it was *The Night Before Christmas* we were writing, and I wanted to ask Mrs. Haley to slow down and I raised my hand and she wouldn't slow down and she wouldn't call on me and so I refused to write. I got in trouble and my parents thought that I had refused to write *The Night Before Christmas* because I was Jewish. I didn't argue. The incident has gone down in my family history as my first political activism.

Please don't spit on us. Please help us.

Christmas was the worst fuck I ever had. She always came too soon. Usually though, she'd make me wait for months, make me count the days, offer me little pieces of chocolate instead of the real thing, watch me cross the days off on the calendar. When she finally did fuck me, she'd present herself as some kind of gift. She'd never give me exactly what I wanted. In the end, after all the buildup and anticipation, we'd both be disappointed, crying among the torn wrappings of our desire.

Please don't fuck us. Spit on us.

I want to burn your bleeping electronic cards. I want to hurl your Santa Claus in a blizzard paperweight. I want to break your Rudolph the Red-nosed Reindeer lapel pins with the stupid nose that blinks. I want to rip the mini Christmas tree ornament earrings from your ears. People feel the need to decorate every possession they own, including their cars. One of my biggest Christmas pet peeves is what I call the holiday hanky code for cars. I've noticed that cars like Mercedes and station wagons have big red ribbons on their front grills, signaling their class status or their family values, while Range Rovers and Jeeps sport the more rugged pine wreath, signaling athleticism and a love of the outdoors. Sometimes though, there are cars with wreaths and a ribbon, I don't know what that signifies, I think they're just confused.

Something else I will never understand is mincemeat pie. What the fuck is mincemeat pie? There's no meat, it isn't like any pie I ever tasted. But do you know what is sounds like? It sounds like pussy. Yeah, like pussy. Like a bunch of butch dyke elves talking, "Mrs. Claus, yeah... she served me up some of her mince meat pie."

Christmas has spit on us. Please help X-mas.

Shame on you, Western Civilization. Cutting down millions of trees each year for the sake of a misappropriated, commercialized pagan celebration is not a ritual we should be proud of. There's an oversized Christmas tree in the foyer of my office building, with empty presents beneath it (what a lovely metaphor), wreaking of pine, a scent that at this point can only remind me of toilet cleanser. It's all I can do to stop myself from sticking a sign on it that simply reads, Yuck.

My boy is seven. It's Christ's birthday.

Christmas gets earlier every year. It's like some imperialistic virus, spreading the killing effects of Christianity and capitalism. Soon Christmas will be all year long. Christmas is the ultimate metaphor for otherness. This is the message of Christmas: You are the wrong religion, you have the wrong family, you have the wrong income, you are the wrong sexuality. You are wrong and you must pay to be right. Right like us. Gotta pay to keep up with the simulacra. Repeat after me, there is no happy family.

Merry X-mas. My boy is spit.

I want to make hard candy cock molds in red and green. I want to dress like Santa and have parents take pictures of their kids sitting on my cock. I want mothers to find their kids sucking on the candy I've offered them, child-heads bobbing on my sticky dick, their greedy little, hungry little tongues lapping at my shiny hardness. I want to fuck Christmas up the ass while it screams, as it always does, faster, harder, more. I want to stab it with a candy cane sucked to sharpened perfection. I want to wrap a string of multi-colored flashing lights around its neck and strangle it as it comes.

I want to go down in history as the girl who killed Christmas.

Christmas Sucks, Again

Hi, my name is Thea and I'm an addict. It's ah, been almost a year, it'll be a year in December, since I did Christmas.

I don't know what made me try it that first time. I mean, I'm a Jew. Jews don't do Christmas. Really, I think that's what makes us more suceptible to addiction, our systems aren't used to Christmas and can't really handle it. Like most self-respecting queers and perverts, Jews didn't grow up having real, good Christmas, and the first time we get a hit, we go down hard. We only have to do it once and we're hooked. I don't know, maybe it was the crowd I was hanging out with, I mean, it seems like everybody does Christmas. And my girlfriend was doing it, so I guess I decided to try it.

So yeah, I do know why I did it. I was also doing true love at the time. And that stuff, that will kill you. You think you can handle it. You think, I'll only do a little bit. You say, on weekends, no big deal, I can stop anytime I want. But it's a lie. That love stuff really gets you. You start hallucinating and living in some alternate reality: you start thinking you're beautiful, the whole world's beautiful, you start liking your neighbors, liking your job, you want to have sex all the time, I mean, everything is out of whack, and yet it seems perfectly normal at the time. You don't realize how far gone you really are. You do a little Christmas on top of true love, and you get really high.

Last year, the Christmas day buzz was really incredible. Add to this the major hit of true love that I was on, and I was a goner. Me and my true love went to this party. Everything seemed so bright, everything was supervivid, loud music, TV blaring, with blinking and flashing lights everywhere, streamers and ribbons of red and green and white. And the host was wearing a '50s style leopard print dress with a bra on the outside. Her girlfriend was wearing a bright red Union Jack suit. And everyone was super friendly. It was like being on ecstacy, but better. On Christmas day, people cooked for hours, dropped by. I lost my sense of space and time and was surprised to find that what had seemed like minutes was actually hours. Pie after pie after pie came steaming out of the oven. People I'd never met before came in and out and became family within the course of a day, within the course of a day with a million courses, we started first homemade crepes, crepes with chocolate, crepes with brie, crepes with jam. The first guests arrived, a teenage girl with huge full breasts and her beautiful sassy mother. The girl was so gorgeous that I couldn't take my eyes off her, and it turned out she was a movie star. Then they left and more people came, and we ate fruit and cookies, and there were gifts and more guests. Everything was soft and wonderful and seemed like a dream. Then there was this aging punk in a rock band with a Hooters t-shirt, and she was in love with me and my girlfriend. She said we were magic. Then again, we were magic, being on both Christmas and true love. Everyone could tell. I think they were getting a contact high off us.

Being on Christmas also made me do things I wouldn't usually do. My true love girlfriend made roast lamb. And you know I must have been really stoned on Christmas and true love, because I started eating meat again that day. It's like that, you start small, thinking, just once, just one Christmas, but it leads to bigger and worse and now I eat meat all the time, always trying to recapture that taste again, that amazing roast lamb that she made, and it didn't stop there: there were salads and vegetables, and then a talent show and the *Wayne's World* lip sync, and the rich photographer and the dyke ex-con from Rykers did some performance in drag where they both ended up half-naked in a heap on the floor and we just about peed ourselves, and then the mother and daughter came back and sang together. And we cried. And the woman with the Hooters shirt loved us some more. And we went home that night. Two girls who barely knew each other but were family.

I mean, it was all so good. I should've have known that sooner or later I'd have to come down. That season, I did so much Christmas that I began to see it everywhere I went, everywhere I looked, Christmas specials on every tv station, decorations at Safeway, on the ATM screen, piped through stores, on the Yahoo home page, and on public transportation. Everywhere. I began to think I was losing my mind. I frantically spent all my money on Christmas, spending money that I didn't have, running up my credit cards just so I could have the best shit available. Add this to the constant emails and plane visits to my long-distance true love, and it all became too much. When I finally hit bottom, I could see that my life had become unmanageable. I was a dual diagnosis addict and had to admit I was powerless over Christmas and true love. Now that I'm in the program and going to synagogue again, I can't believe I didn't see the signs.

I don't think it's just residual paranoia from all that Christmas I did, but now I see the link between the 12 days of Christmas and the 12-step program. And all the people who commit suicide on Christmas… does anyone consider that maybe these people overdosed on Christmas? And what about the fact that if you unscramble the word Noel that it spells lone?

I now see my addiction as part of a national epidemic rather than a personal pathology. Having had a spiritual awakening as the result of the 12 Steps, I am trying to carry this message to others and to practice these principles in all my affairs. I want to tell you that Christmas and true love are deadly for queers and other freaks: these hegemonic constructs are about conformity, about acceptance, about maintaining status quo. And the more we try to achieve these ideals, the more we destroy ourselves in the process. Now I know that true love and Christmas in all their forms, love songs, Christmas songs, are all a big conspiracy designed to keep us paying through the nose for the right to remain compliant, alienated, and poor.

This season is a lot different than last. I have a lot more money and lot more free time to spend it. Alone. Because now that my true love is gone, the only drug I'll be doing is Ex-Miss. And this December 25th, the holiday methodone clinic will be at my place, just me and my Jewish friends watching movies and eating Chinese takeout. Now that I'm not doing Christmas anymore, I'm just trying to hold on until the next High Holidays.

IV

Chevy Malibu
Racing downhill without brakes
Taught me to let go

Dear Elizabeth

I dreamed about you again last night. I could tell you this over orange juice, but the thing is we both know that's not it. And you were a metaphor and Peter is always there; phantom Peter who gets made up but always gets a reference. See, this is what I'm trying to tell you, but I know you understand. It's not easy, indeterminacy, but it's worth it. Indeterminacy is dusk, the buildings on my block are pink, but the point is the moment, not the color. It is some dawns, during spring, remembering by mistake the solitude of city early mornings. The politics of indeterminacy are so muddy when you're queer. But it's even worse when everyone else is queer.

It's all in the way you engage and appreciate. See, I appreciate. Just because someone is smart and beautiful doesn't mean you have to fuck them.

Girls break my heart often. They don't know the difference between love and holding. I want a girl who beholds me. And most of them can't. It's as if embracing the term dyke means women are simply the other side of men; no one is safe anymore and all terrain is dangerous.

Girls break my heart often. My first memory of being queer. I'm four, playing on the handrail at preschool. My heart wrings and twists at the sight of a little girl, younger than me, in a pink dress. I want to squeeze her so hard it hurts.

I dream about Jana. The stain from her sweaty dress ruined my couch and it's what's left. That night we left Litterbox and stumbled, shrieking into Ringold Alley where the leather boys trick in the quiet dark. Jana shoved me up against the cyclone fence, pushed her hips against mine. I laughed and turned my head. She slept in my bed that night. I wouldn't fuck her. I wanted to be friends forever. With Jana, I'd finally met my match. She'd gone out with Don DeLillo, simply by writing him a letter. Gorgeous and brilliant and funny, she would call me and we'd talk for hours on the phone, analyzing books, girls, culture. We passed puns back and forth like Japanese ping pong pros. I was in heaven.

February 24, 1997. Yesterday I tried to set some lame-ass boundary and told Jana not to call till late afternoon because I had to take a nap and in my dream she calls anyway and in my dream she kisses me, sticking her tongue in my mouth and I push her away and then grab her and we kiss really deeply and it felt so real and then my mom catches us.

Girls get in so deep. That's why I'm queer. It's not that they're any sexier than men, it's that they break my heart better.

Jana lies to me, by omission, and Jana tells me the truth. We went to Josie's to eat two days ago and for the first time we couldn't connect. I kept wondering what I said wrong. Then I remembered she'd done heroin the night before. Then I started thinking about all those times on the phone we'd be talking and she'd drop the phone and start puking uncontrollably and I never knew why and I was so sympathetic and I just thought she got sick a lot. Her friend Liz's nose is collapsing from the inside, collapsing on itself. Jana's therapist fires her because she does drugs and I listen to her sob for two hours and I cry because she's hurting and I love her. And the next day she calls me from jail, bailing out the girl she did the H with, the girl with the girlfriend, whose girlfriend put the TRO out on her, and I'm going through all this with her, wishing I didn't feel anything because somehow now that I know all these life's ups and downs are about drugs, I feel duped. Like they are going to happen over and over again, like it's not some life process but rather a repetition, endless, till she breaks out of it and I don't want to hurt for her every time something else crappy happens.

Went to dinner with Jana tonight. When she sees people she knows she tells them she's having a hard time and she's feeling better. She still hurts, her whole body hurts, and she's jumpy and pale, red-eyed, breaking out in boils and I realize as I write this that it breaks my heart. She hasn't been able to smell or taste anything lately. I had to stop myself from asking her if she could smell the nightblooming jasmine because she wouldn't be able to.

Jana tells me I don't need someone like Manya who always has a monkey on her back and she says, "You gotta feel sorry for her. It's so tough. I know how it is to have that monkey," and I wonder if she knows what she has just said.

After dinner, Jana and I buy this leather jacket and pants from a junkie who's selling off her stuff. She says she's leaving town, but you can tell she needs a fix. I buy the jacket. Jana really wants it after she sees it on me. She says she'll trade me anything of hers I want. I keep it. Until I get it home and reach in the pocket and pull out a used syringe. I give Jana the jacket.

I go out to bars and come home close to tears, feeling drunk with easy emotion. Most times, I go over the evening in my head and realize I didn't even drink. Girls go to the same place as alcohol. I throw them up at the end of the night so I can drink more. Sometimes, I do Patrón shots, tequila cutting the blade of girls who look away. It's what they do. Sadly. Look away. Gay men pass and then look back. Girls pass and look away and never look back. I haven't learned yet not to smile.

Melinda says she can't be my friend anymore because when we get close, she likes me as more than a friend. And even though she is dating someone else, she still has feelings for me. She wants distance. I want to kill her for stealing yet one more best friend. Friends. How hard. Some. Some like berries and some like fruit trees, grafting, careful, years of barrenness. And some. So hard. Hard like pointing to my own organs and saying that's why and this is how.

The moment of beholding isn't. Isn't linear. Isn't going anywhere. Beholding hovers, invisible to the naked eye, circling like a halo, flying away, drawn in, everywhere impossible to locate: a valence. The electron's unrequited passion for the atom: again and always.

Sincerely.

Dear #85

Dear Jill:

I can't do it. I can't even say you. It's too close. I'll say her. But it's you. I can't say it because I want you. And I shouldn't. You are very dangerous. For me, dangerous starts with a J. Jesse, Jill. When names become words, signifiers. When a girl has ceased to be a real person but the creation exists, twisted, active, like a fungus, like a yeast infection, conjugating Jesse: To Jesse, Used to Jesse, Jesse will Jesse, I Jesse, You Jesse, We all Jesse, To Jesse someone off. And so the able-bodied noun sublimates into an ethereal, ubiquitous verb.

I hate the cabbies in Walnut Creek. But you. Sweaty long-haired, what, 18-year-old guy, you close the door for me. I watch you slide yourself into the car and like a stop-action slo-mo, click, click, click, the wind catches the long hair, click, the wind pushes the mesh football jersey against you, click, against your chest, click, against your breasts, click click click click click. I settle back and smile, smugly, out the window.

She's nervous already. I decide it's a she, searching for the medallion with the name on it so can know for sure. There isn't one. Maybe it's because she's only been driving a cab for three weeks. Gets lost. Apologizes for the sap on the windshield. Some truck cuts us off, she swears at him and then apologizes to me for her language. I suggest rubbing alcohol. For the windshield. Her hoarse voice speaks of life lived too hard too young. She's been sober six months she says. She's from the South, with that easy kick-back confidence, even though she's nervous, that dykes cultivate for years. A natural. We pass one of Walnut Creek's three homeless. "Shit, the pop tarts are in the trunk. I get to keep this car. Drive it around." Like 16, you know, she's proud and turning to quick look, smile, flashing her heartbreaker grin, the Marlboro scar on the side of her face.

After several calls to base, we get to Rossmoor. Taking it one step further, because although I've already decided I'm still not sure, I ask for her cab number so I can call her for the ride back to BART. #85. Jill, she says. Nice to meet you. Yep.

Way back. Asks how my time with Gram was. Tells me the sap isn't sap but Coke. Her ex threw a Coke at her car last night. Yep. I mean, if that's not lesbian…Asks me what clubs I go to. Junk, Red. G-spot, she says. Outing herself. Tells me she'll take me out. Tells me she can drive out to San Francisco.

Dear Danny:

I can't believe I didn't tell you about Jill, #85. Number 85. I wanted to write the letter to her, but I couldn't—I don't even want to get that close. Jill. I wasn't even sure if she was a girl until I heard her say her name, even though I'd been in her cab for twenty minutes. Twenty minutes because she got lost on the way to Rossmoor. She was incredible, this one. What a fantasy—14-year-old boy from the South, sweaty and bragging, long straggly hair, limp, hanging around her face, that scar next to her eye, one arm on the wheel, the other resting along the back of the seat. Just like a date, except me in the back seat. And it's been months, right? Months since anyone's really flirted with me and here she is, nervous, the more nervous she is, the more confident I get. She's young and I'm not; she's a boy and I'm a girl—in the back seat, the customer. Okay, so I'm falling quick for the raspy, 12-Step laugh, the nervous cocksure backward glances.

So on the way back, I'm feeling somewhat like an adultress or something like some sultry Kathleen Turner older woman. She shows me her new purchase—some funky bong pot thing, like I'd even know. I ask if that gets in the way of her sobriety, and get this, she says it's all she can do to keep from puking everyday. Really. She says, I used to be fat and was bulemic for two years and I still throw up every morning, even if I don't try to. My doctor says my heart could stop at any minute. It helps me not to puke. Except I haven't puked in two weeks, ever since I broke up with my girlfriend. She passes back her pager number and tells me she'll come to San Francisco to take me out. Whatever reasons I have for not dating Lynn evaporate. This girl makes Lynn look like a model girlfriend, an honor roll student.

I can't do it. I can't do it. I really can't do it. Right?

Yours.

Dear Diane

It's true. Someone shattered the china house. Knocked over the metronome. Kicked the warm dog. Bit the fragile cup. But your holes sing to me even as you ache.

Sweet unfinished and unfinishing, shards are dangerous but so attractive to kindred flesh. Some need to be cut to talk and then some, like me, need to talk to be cut, so I don't live on the gold coast of Connecticut. Or Boston. Eileen's deficient swims in the cool waters off the coast, targeting bullion in sunken galleys and secret holds, tight with silence and longing. The fish lie, Di, and are never your friend.

Spotted girl, red spiked collars fall on deaf eyes, wasted, until Jamaica pond flowers. And it will. And it does. Contrary to popular opinion, spring is not a yearly event. Although some would have us think so and still others set their clocks by its appearance. I watch time-honored machinations but prefer to be surprised by lightness and the smell of trees. Sometimes spring takes years to come. Sometimes spring is often and multiple. Most often spring arrives, a letter in the mail, that I don't even need to open. You.

Love.

Dear Em

What's the hardest thing you can think of? Dear Em. Divide it by
two. Dear Em. Don't think twice. Dear Em. Confuse me again, why
don't you. Dear Em. Don't scare me like that. Dear Em. God you
make me mad. Dear Em. Why don't you count every little second
and every little grain of sand and every little piece of rice and if it
isn't even, don't ever leave me, dear Em. What if it isn't even, dear
Em? What if I need you more than you need me? What if you give
me more than you get from me? What if, dear Em.

Dear Em:
I'm sorry that sometimes I get bored with your stories. I am sorry I
get bored because maybe I'm worried your story was longer. Maybe
your story was one second longer than mine. Maybe your story was
one thing and mine was many. Maybe I just want you to be proud of
me. Maybe you mean more to me than any pretty theory. Maybe
impressing you is better than that new girl I imagined. Maybe.

Dear Em:
Maybe we have until next week to be friends. Maybe this phone call
is the last. Maybe we have until infinity. Maybe I have all the moments
in a sitting bowl waiting to hear you and maybe you have many
basketfuls to say.

Dear Em:
Your hair is long short mine. Dear Em. I do you yoga. Dear Em. I
want to change you the world. Girls who think themselves
opposite have an awful lot in common.

Dear Em:
A dog's funeral is the way to find a friend.

Dear Kate

It is a rather day.

When name becomes poem.

You know you're deep in postmodern trouble when the lightning flash turns your window into a computer screen, rather than the other way around. San Francisco is dramatic tonight and we should be making love to it, blue light making our sex neon and momentary. We should be glowing electric and instead my lights flash and surge and I would unplug my computer but then how would I write to you? The connection would be lost and what's a little surge? Lost among larger more pleasurable tightenings and clenchings.

Can you tell I miss you? Can you feel it so far off?

Oh to be in prison with you.

I smell of soft cotton and the right one is nothing interesting, but the left, ah Kate, the left you would love tonight. I ran and caught one trolley, five buses, and three trains today. Kate, I parked one car and cooked one meal and ate one carton of Hazelnut Godiva in two sittings. I went to court twice and made two deadlines. I sweat a lot today, Kate, and dream of the day I end a day like this with you, smelling my day and making love to the running, rather than the spacious and distant telling.

I carried Genet and dried flowers and kissed the book and thought about carrying it with me always but it is such a heavy book. How do strangers feel about Genet?

I read about Ryni tonight and about Broca's Aphasia and contralateral motor control.

It is thundering and raining, Kate. We must be together in rain soon.

I read about all the ways the school will not accommodate Ryni. Read about lesions and empty speech and misarticulations. "Substitution of one word for another such as table for chair are common." This was for Wernicke's Aphasia.

One girl's paralysis is another girl's poetry.

Word-finding difficulty. I know it well. Also known as being in love. Speechless. Being a poet.

When all I can write
Is your name as a poem
My pen breathes easy

Kate.

My fingers long to sign to you. Yet one more way speech fails and the body knows. Teach me to speak with my hands, Kate. Kate, love is the failure of sense and technology. Madness.

I am disordered for you and love you madly.

Dear Matthew

It was the only place, driving across country and back, that I had been scared to go—Laramie. I wanted to visit the fence, the place where you were killed. I wanted to be out for you, to mark your murder, to demonstrate to whomever I asked for directions that the world remembers and that you were. A gay pilgrimage of sorts. Your mom, "I'm not sure I ever will."

No Vacancy signs flashing. Late July and Laramie's annual rodeo was in full swing. I hate rodeos. I went to one once with my girlfriend Sandra. She was a huge strong firefighter. Only way she felt safe going to a rodeo was to pass as a man and she did and people "sirred" her and all was fine but I was terrified someone would recognize her as a girl and us as dykes and be really pissed that we had fooled them. I feel like a Jew at rodeos. I mean I am a Jew but at those moments I really feel it like at any moment I will be recognized and rounded up and taken away. My people, whoever they are, don't do rodeos.

I saw you last night, in *People* magazine: "On Oct. 7, 1998, Judy and Dennis Shepard's son Matthew, 21, a gay University of Wyoming student, was beaten, tied to a wooden fence outside Laramie and left on the windblown prairie to die." What, was it a gay university? Your assailants at least got roofer Russell Henderson and the lesser, high school dropout Aaron McKinney, but not straight roofer and straight dropout. So the caption says you were a poli-sci major. And your dad says he comes from "trailer trash, travelling construction workers."

My travelling companion, Daf, hadn't even wanted to drive through Laramie, let alone stay there one night. We were taking four days to get back to California, driving 12-hour days to get across the country, arriving somewhere between 10 p.m. and 12 a.m. each night at our crappy Motel 6 accommodations, which shouldn't have been a problem because we had done this all the way across the country and our crappy Motel 6 rooms had been guaranteed months ago. But, as I'm sure you know, the rodeo is a big deal in Laramie, and some asshole motel clerk had sold our room out from under us. So there we were, two Jewish dykes with dyed hair and facial piercings, according to *People* magazine, at 10:30 p.m., with a storm brewing and every hotel for miles around booked solid. And the desk clerk at the Motel 6, definitely family, wouldn't help us get another room. And to top it all off, he gave us attitude, catty bitch.

In between calls to Motel 6 customer service and AAA and neighboring towns, I called Kate. I had been waiting since yesterday to call her. She had called the day before when I was driving, on our way to night two, Ohio, and this was to be our first phone conversation. She had called the day before but Daf wouldn't let me talk because I wasn't allowed to talk when I was driving but Daf said Kate had a sexy phone voice and Kate had called right as we were talking about her, me saying how amazing she was and me saying maybe she's probably not even thinking about me and right then the phone rings and it's her. And she said she just had this overwhelming desire to say hi. Daf translated for me and I told her I'd call the next day because it would be too late when we get in to Ohio. And so I call her the next night in the middle of this fight with Motel 6 and Kate says she didn't call the day before because she had an overwhelming desire to say hi but rather she was thinking about me and thought I was amazing and we talked for just a minute about being on the road and she said she pictured me with the world passing by me as I drove and I told her about the torrential rains we had had to pull over for and she said, "I love when weather stops things," and my heart, clean like rain, swelled.

So eight calls to Motel 6 proved fruitless and AAA saved the day and got us a room at some place called the Camelot Inn and we drove a couple of hours, trying to get there as fast as we could because the old guy proprietor of the Camelot Inn said he didn't want any partyers staying at his place. Daf told him we weren't partyers, we just wanted to sleep. When we got there, we had to ring the bell, which rang into the room behind the desk, the house, really, of this very elderly couple. And the woman was glad we hadn't gotten there too late because her husband was sick and she didn't want him staying up too late because it wasn't good for his health. We asked for a room on the first floor because I had a body-bag sized duffel and she gave us the handicapped room, even though that's illegal but who else was going to arrive after 12:30 a.m., and it was the largest single room I have ever seen in my life and we met the old couple's dog on the way to our room, the dog with one eye. There was a chill in the air. We had just driven through the heatwave where 88 people had died in two weeks. The breeze, heaven.

Confused about where I was and sick with stomach pains for the third day in a row, I woke up the next morning, threw a sweatshirt over my pajamas and searched for a pay phone, couldn't find one and had to go to the gas station down the way. I called my parents to see if they had any idea what to do about my stomach because my dad had stomach problems and he said Mylanta. I mean, Mylanta, of course. And I told Dad I had met someone, not that he wanted to hear it, but I couldn't help myself. And I talked really quietly because there were all these cowboys in oversized trucks stopping for gas in this weird town where every building was spiffed up with faux pioneer storefront facades. The general store/gas station was out of antacid.

So I went to the grocery and then I went back to the Camelot and the old woman asked me how I had slept and there she was in the laundry room folding sheets with her husband. They did all the work at the Camelot Inn, they were the front desk, the maid, and everything else here and they were at least 80 years old and they had saved us the night before and made us welcome. And it was cold in Wyoming, and windy, and tomorrow we would be in Nevada and the next day home.

Love.

Dear Mrs. Porter, or Ms. Porter, Probably

This letter is to you because you are the scariest part of me, the scariest thing I can think of. Wanna be my pen pal? I want to get to know you. Seventh grade was a hard time. And then again in tenth grade, was it?

Anyway, you must be wondering why I am contacting you after all these years. What made me think of you? I was in the shower, filling my travel bottle of shampoo as I prepare to go work on a farm with my lover this weekend, and I remembered to squeeze the air out, like you told us to do before plane trips because air expands at higher altitudes, and I've always done it and nothing has ever exploded in my luggage. Thanks. And I started thinking that so many things about the everyday that I do come from you. Like tossing salt in boiling water to lower the boiling point. Or not mixing medications in containers because they can chemically react with each other. Or how it's bad if oven cleaner smells good because the gases really are noxious and it's good if they smell that way. I mean, countless things. And in my head, when I think, or not think, but heed these lessons, I kind of think, but not think, about you. I kind of don't think about you because I am ashamed. I got excited about science. You noticed. You recognized me because you loved science, too. But I was scared, terrified, still am, about what else you may have recognized.

You. Huge breasts, kinky hair, angry, so bitter. Smart and so disliked; right, but so embattled. Always on the righteous, losing side. And those crazy clothes you wore from when? The '60s? '70s? Or did no one but you ever wear those clothes? And the way your spit rattled in your mouth as you talked. Thick and white, it flew between your teeth, lips—sometimes staying attached, venturing out but with enough surface tension to return to your mouth—or other times, flinging itself in great globs on a student's desk. That stuff really travelled.

God, and there was the time you were saying something to me in class, what, congratulating me for a correct answer, and you spit on me, on my desk, but also in my eye, and all I could do was look at you, not looking at the spit on my desk or wiping my eye. And all the other kids saw, but like somehow I needed to be an ally to you. And that's what was scary. Maybe this is all a projection. And maybe someday you'll tell me it's all true. But I knew what it was like to be you.

I'd been monstrous before. Grotesque. Was. Is. Out. On the outs. The outside. And later, out. It's so scary. Were you scared a lot? And did you see that in me, too? Did you recognize it? How scary to be your friend. How scary to defend you to kids, parents.

And you recommended me for the recombinant DNA and cloning seminar at UOP. A summer camp for nerds. The only people on campus were the summer dummies (incoming freshpeople who got in on condition of passing summer school) and us, the 10th-grade nerds, who were more adept at school and earning better grades than these "dummies" could ever hope to. You know, so it was really great and kind of emphasized the weird freak thing.

I'm really just scared to be the monster of the minute. Whatever society deems monstrous at that minute. Because even though the minute is fleeting, the effects last a lifetime and you never forget, do you? And even if they don't remember to make you one, you do it yourself. You've learned and you remember. You carry the freak in your purse, in your heart, and to every new person you meet, you say, "Hello, I am a freak. Nice to meet you." And you hope it will be different this time, but it's already too late.

Too late. Too late for us. How are you? Too late for the sad boys from Littleton. I know. I know. I know. Sssh, come here. And, I'm sorry. I want to tell the boys, I hope you're really cool in heaven because you must have gone through hell down here. I don't even believe in heaven or hell, but I remember high school.

Take care.

Poetics

Music is not music until it is heard. — John Cage

Kris,

Saturday the sunflowers wilted before they bloomed

Poisoned by the venomous girls of the night who will

fuck you or kill you depending on the light

The completed circle gives the illusion of wholeness

Practice makes imperfect

Really, I'd like to think I'd let anything be a poem. But probably, it's
anything that sounds harsh, takes me by surprise, or knocks me
on my ass in some way or another

Abstraction = death

Actually, for people whose sexuality has long been controlled by
outside forces, the choice of whom to sleep with and the ability
to articulate these choices is an actualization of freedom

How alone do you get

It takes people different amounts of time to climb my three flights

So why not read the piece and not CARE

Blue lake green beans

I need more friends who will let me keep my hands in my pants

They never would have called O'Hara's work campy if he wasn't
a fag

The word sex is not erotic

They should outlaw poets from using words like flesh, blood, bone
and only sometimes on special occasions like when

company's over allow them to use orange

I tough god

Sunflower is certainly verboten

When touch becomes tough

Think with your liver

I do think poems that reach me are ones that seem written for me

The me being the most alive part of any of us

Fuck as a figure of speech

Elbow is erotic

Erotic = power
Poetry is not poetry until it is heard
Glue gun is erotic
Write me
Love, Thea

V

Whose paisley jacket?
And that noose around her neck
She is lost downtown

To the One I Haven't Met Yet

The girl smoking outside the ballet studio stands, hip jutting out, her feet in fourth position.

They demolished my neighbors' house today. I tell Krista that they demolished the benches because homeless people were living there. There is caution tape and signs surrounding the area, now only a three-sided trench on the ground. No forwarding address. It was begging to be lived in, says Krista. This is why I love her.

Twice in the last week on the 22 line I have witnessed people fighting over whether or not they are disabled and should be sitting in the front of the bus. This is an ugly fight. Someone gets pissed off and tells someone else they aren't disabled and shouldn't be sitting in those seats when all sorts of elderly people are standing because the bus is so crowded. And then the person being accused replies, loud and indignant, that they are disabled, not as young as they look, have a card in their wallet saying they are disabled, can read the sign, have a brain tumor. And they doth protest too much and it appears they are lying, but it's too late now the hole has been dug. Now they have to be disabled. And somewhere, somehow they are, you know. And what an awful thing to have to prove. And what an awful thing to be, out there policing who sits in the disabled seats on the bus, for the good of mankind, for godsakes.

I don't know. I've started giving out change again when people ask.

And the sculptor on the bus who invited me to get my hands dirty.

And the cab driver who gave me a ride for free when I had no money.

The three-sided trench is filled in with cement.

She answered the phone and I said, "Sorry, I must have dialed the wrong number."

And she said, "Maybe not."

Bus

I'm in my usual seat in the back of the 22 Fillmore. Two men make their way to the back, their loud voices and strong cologne precede them to their seats, right in front of me. One of them starts in with the young girl who is already sitting there reading a book. "Hi. What are you studying? How old are you?"

The girl responds with short polite answers, not lifting her head from the book. This smells bad; I look out the window, not wanting to give these guys any attention.

"Seventeen, huh? When I was 17, I was in jail learning how to strangle someone with a broom handle. Wish I had been in school. Where are you going? To study? With friends, huh? Are they girls or boys?"

I want to stop these guys from harassing this girl, but I'm not really sure she can't do it herself. I want to assume she could stop them if she wanted to. The men are older, though, and relentless.

"My friend says I should get my nipple pierced. What do you think? Should I get my nipple pierced?" She shrugs. "Okay, who do you think is cuter, me or my friend?" She doesn't reply. "Come on, who? It's me, right?" She mumbles something about not wanting to answer, then abruptly packs up her stuff and gets off the bus.

I can't even look at these guys, I'm so disgusted. I don't believe it, but the loud one starts with me, "What do you think?"

"I think you're obnoxious."

"Just because I was talking to that girl? I think that was her stop. I don't think she got off the bus just because of me."

"I think you were trying to make her uncomfortable."

"What, because I was talking to her about my nipple?" He turns to his friend. "Do you think I was trying to make her uncomfortable?" His friend thinks for a moment, then replies slowly, unconvincingly, "I... don't think you were trying to make her... uncomfortable."

At this moment the bus stops as it loses its connection to the overhead electric wires. The loud guy looks to his friend, "Hey, let's get out here." They jump out the back door. I know that wasn't their stop. They got off of the bus because of me. I think I made them uncomfortable.

MUNI

A young man lopes and darts through the crowded MUNI train. Shiny and thin like fiberglass, his hair seems to grow from the air instead of his head. He stops next to a man in a suit, sinks to his knees, wraps his arms around the man's legs, lays his head against the man's thigh. The man in the suit looks around, shocked, then

pats the young man clinging to him

or

punches the young man clinging to him

or

kisses the young man clinging to him.

The young man gets up, walks through the train car, kneels, wraps his arms around yet another stranger.

He is somebody's son.

He is somebody's failure.

He is somebody's savior.

MUNI 2

We are packed in as usual, hip against genitals against briefcase against thigh. Each exhalation is someone's inhalation. At Civic Center we watch as yet one more person squeezes in. He's a tall man with matted hair and clothes so old they are colorless. He disappears himself against the train wall, leaning against the bar that opens the doors, which close and open, close and open, close and open in response to his weight. The train doesn't move. A voice comes over the intercom telling whomever it is to stop leaning on the bar. The voice says it three times, the doors closing and opening, closing and opening. Finally, the man, who seems not to understand the voice but rather the weight of many blaming eyes, steps off the train. The doors close.

The train progresses to the next station. Someone a few bodies away quips, "That's what I call a win–win situation." People laugh.

At the last stop, I approach the man I think made the comment. He is white and wears red boxing gloves around his neck. "Did you make that comment?" I ask.

"Why?" he asks. "Do I look like someone who would make that kind of comment?"

I answer, "I thought it came from your direction, and it really bothered me that everyone laughed."

"It wasn't me," he answers, "and sometimes you have to laugh or else you'll cry."

BART

Alive and soaring after Poetry for the People at Glide, I'm on the escalator at Civic Center Station BART when I hear it. I can hear it before I can see it, before I'm even on the platform. I don't even hear it, I feel it in my chest: a man being an asshole, a man being out of control. When I get to the platform, I see a woman being chased in circles around the benches and columns by a leering man, "What's that stain on your shirt, baby? Why you wearing such a short skirt? How'd you get those stains on your shirt?" She is crying and running. Her friend is begging him to stop. The rest of the crowded platform is watching and silent. I go upstairs and call the police. They tell me they are busy with another call in the system.

When I return he is still chasing the hysterical woman. No one is doing anything to stop him. I look around for people to help me help her. I want to form a group of people to get him away from her. I look at a woman who looks like a lesbian, she looks away. At the other end of the platform, a man yells, "Leave her alone." I join him and yell the same thing to the man.

Irate, the man approaches me, screaming at me about being a dyke, telling me how he's going to fuck me and how his cock is going to go right through me, how all a cunt like me needs is to be fucked by a real man. He's right in my face and I just keep nodding at him. He doesn't want to fight me, though, because fighting a woman is weak. He decides he wants to find the man, "the pussy," who yelled at him first.

The train finally arrives, but the doors don't open. Right then, a white guy in white shorts pushes the man against the wall, kicks his legs apart and begins to frisk him. A black woman in bright, mixed-up, mismatched clothes carrying a full black garbage bag asks the guy in white shorts if he wants her to handle the arrest. He's got it, he says. A blue army of bullet-proof-vest-wearing cops floods the escalators, descends the stairs to the platform. I board the train, shaking. The two women sit across from me and we don't talk.

Walgreens

This is the third time I have called aside the pharmacist to complain. They continue to shelve the Vaseline next to the condoms, along with all the other lubricants. With a line of gay men waiting behind me, I explain, this time to the manager, that Vaseline eats through latex and is not a suitable lubricant for safe sex. The fact that they place the Vaseline next to lubricants and condoms implies that it is safe, when in fact it could be life-threatening. The men behind me chime in with "Right on" and "She's right" and "Yeah, and it's murder to wash out of your sheets."

Safeway

Waiting in line at Safeway, a
> magician
> fag
> homeless man

in front of me turns around, and asks like we're best friends and have been swapping secrets for hours, "Do you think it's okay to have milk and meat on a Friday? My father was Roman Catholic and it's Friday and I know he would just kill me."

He shows me his meal of ham, cream cheese, and a loaf of bread. He has old makeup on his face, barrettes in his hair, sparkles on his eyelids, and wears tattered, wildly colored clothing and shoes with glitter on them. We dish, him telling me about the gorgeous man he met on BART today. He tells me he invited the man to visit. He excludes my male friend from the conversation with "This is girl talk." He likes me too, he says, and invites me to visit him anytime where he lives, the bushes behind Davies Medical Center.

Baby

A homeless man
    white man
    black man
maneuvers a stroller from the back of the bus, apologizing as he rolls
over people's feet, thanking me as I hold the back door open for him.
I glance at the baby. It is
    white
    blue
    laughing.

Flower

Ivy and I are walking up Market Street. We hear wailing behind us. We look and it's a

> young woman
> little girl
> wicked witch

sitting on steps, sobbing into her hands. We feel for her immediately.

"Let's buy her a flower," Ivy says. We hurry to a flower shop a few blocks away, buy a pink Gerber daisy and carry it back.

Before we reach the place where we saw her, we hear fighting. It's her. She runs in our direction. I take a step toward her.

"Ugly fucking dykes," she growls.

Not sure if she means us, I joke, "Don't be mean to us, we want to give you a flower."

Looking directly at me, she replies, "You can shove your fucking flower up your fucking ass."

Boys

Walking through Duboce Park on a dark Friday night. A group of
   skateboarders
   lost boys
   panhandlers
are hanging out, laughing, pissing at the curb. I walk by, furious.
   "Well, hello to you too," they taunt me as I pass.
   "The world is not your fucking toilet," I reply. Later I think of
myself as a little dog who takes on the big dog world, not knowing
how small he is.

Man

A man gets out of a
  van
  cab
  limo.
He wears hospital pajamas and a parka, his face red and hair graying.
He lurches to a building, leans awkwardly, trying to open the metal
gate with a key, hold his cane, and toss three plastic bags through the
gate to the foyer. He's almost falling down in his effort, collapsing.
He is
  out of control
  all alone
  coming home.

Animals I Have Known

You told me the story on my first day of training to be a community organizer. You watched the project kids throwing rocks at a bird, torturing and finally killing it. You ran away crying hysterically.

The super of 312 East 21st says, "You aren't from this neighborhood. You don't know these people. I know these people. They're animals. Doing drugs. They're monsters."

In the rain, two little damp animals, a tiny bird, a small mouse. I stop and watch them for a moment. Panting, dying from rat poison, eyes frantic. I can see their hearts beating fast in their bodies. Hurriedly, I continue on.

There's piss in the hallways. Shit on the stairwells. "Body decayed in the basement once."

Trying to avoid the super on East 21st, I pass by a group of Black Hebrews. I am assaulted by their megaphone rhetoric as "evil white men" quickly changes to "evil white women" for my benefit. On my right a man threatens, "I'm gonna rape you."

Syringes litter the abusive concrete corners. A kitten mews in a dark stairwell. My heart goes out to it. I want to tuck it in my jacket, make it safe, take it home.

Kids

Kids are getting out of school and I am waiting for the #3 train at the Utica Station. I haven't been out to the neighborhood yet, my backpack pulls heavy on my shoulders, and I am already exhausted. I want to sit down. The only seats now available are at the end of the platform, where some black teenage boys are sitting up on the backs of the benches, talking and playing. The end of the platform is considered dangerous because fewer people wait there, mostly because there are drivers in the front and middle of the train, never at the end. I consider for a moment and then go to sit. The boy next to me looks over and says to himself, "She sat next to me." Then, kind of wonderingly, "You sat next to me."

"Yep," I reply.

Astonished, "Don't I look dangerous?"

"No. Are you dangerous?"

"No, I'm nice and sweet."

The Ones We Have To Fear

"You got lucky,"
Says white-boy, radical-activist-from-Brooklyn Lenny
Lucky, he says, that I was never raped
You know, white-organizer-woman in black
Crown Heights, Brooklyn

Did I get lucky that day
Eight years old, waiting at the rec center
For Jessica's mom
To pick us up,
When a white man flashed me
Made me climb a tree
So he could see my underwear
(I still remember apologizing to him
Because I couldn't climb
As high as he wanted me to)
Did I get lucky that day
When he traumatized me so that I remember
Everything that happened
Remember the design on his t-shirt
The mouse with the woman shrieking "eeek"
A long extended line of e's before the k
Remember looking at mug shots, being asked to testify
To identify him
The gun they found in his car
Remember everything
Except
His
Penis?

Did I get lucky that day
When I talked to him because
He was a

Jogger
White
And reminded me of my
Father?
Breaking my trust of all safe white men
At the age of eight?

We know the facts
The majority of rapes of women are by their boyfriends or husbands
We stick to our own class, race—just like they do.

So, white boy sitting next to me in class
It is you I have to fear
It is you I have to educate
Because you got lucky.

Grace

Skinny weave-braids
Swinging against your ageless skull
Mother of many
Up four steep flights
No boiler
I smoke and I vote
Putting your teeth in
For important meetings
So you look pretty
For the politicians or
The comm-uuu-ni-tee board

Speaking slow
Speaking proud
Of
Laura
Pee Wee
Ryan
And all the others
Your kids, their kids
Kids of kids-in-law
All in one hot blue apartment
Each new birth
Welcome
Joyous

San Francisco Chronicle, 7/8/98

Dead Girls' Mother Held
Reassembling what has been scattered
Poetry is peace that's shelled

We hold truth, suffocation-swelled
Whose arms are the ones that mattered
Dead girls' mother held

Outrage embraced and race misspelled
Expert words on newsprint splattered
Poetry is peace that's shelled

Moments guess when and how she yelled
Above the haze and highs that clattered
Dead girls' mother held

In what small lives, three bodies felled
Despaired apartment, sorrow spattered
Poetry is peace that's shelled

Hold and rock the abbreviated world
Where remorse is noted, reported then shattered
Poetry is peace that's shelled
Dead girls' mother held

Lorena

You were the first person I met in Crown Heights, on my first day out in the neighborhood. It was raining. You offered me a towel and proudly showed me the clear vial that contained the jiggling 26 feet of *rubbah* you had recently reamed from your colon.

You witnessed a stabbing. Two men you knew. At the fish market on your block. One friend killed another with scissors. There was blood all over. You were shaken up for days.

I missed it by a matter of minutes. You said it was fate, that I wasn't supposed to see this. You thank me, "You're doing more for them than they're doing for themselves." You feed me fresh pear, send me out with an apple.

I see you on the sidewalk in front of the market. Rushing before sundown. We share the same sabbath. We hug like old friends. We kiss good-bye. You tell me I'm getting fat, like my grandmother used to do. You tell me you love me when we hang up the phone.

After a planning meeting as I'm leaving your house, you tell me I'm becoming a New Yorker, I should marry a Trumpish, and you'll be my housekeeper. How else are you going to get your big house, you ask me. Sickened, I try to laugh, wondering if it's a joke or glimpses of structures unseen we have chosen to ignore.

We're late for a meeting with Assemblyman Green. We argue. Angry, you tell me, "You think because I am Black, I am stupid!" And you didn't just say it once. I couldn't even continue fighting. All of a sudden I didn't know what we were arguing about. I didn't want to take it personally, but I started crying. I couldn't stop. Your sister yelled at you and comforted me.

Ours is a friendship burdened with other people's garbage. When I first came into the neighborhood, you told me your biggest issue was race relations, the tension between Blacks and Jews. Looks like we have to clean house.

City Sestina

And this is the city
Where dogs play on roofs
Dog shit footprints skid dirty sidewalks
Sarah and I take walks and cry because we're friends
I want to hand out blankets
And the city is my text

When everything's a text
Art rolls like fog over the city
Moments are colored as if with paint or conceptual blankets
Vision shifts, I see people naked on their roofs
The woman who lives below me is not my friend
And I feel close to my neighbors who make their homes on the
sidewalk

Here the written page is the sidewalk
Stickers gum spray paint piss and puke write the text
The ones who read poems in it are my friends
The ones loving in, not despite, the city
Living in studios partying on their roofs
Serenading the stars huddling together sharing blankets

This is the city where I gave away a blanket
To a man who walked up to me on the sidewalk
He'd been hiding from rain under overhanging roofs
Nervous I'd read his request as the same homeless text
We hear over and over in the city
Instead we introduced ourselves shook hands parted friends

Sometimes I feel like I have no friends
I turn to my books my cats my old baby blanket
Security and warmth come from different places in the city
Seeing acquaintances in the market greeting as we pass on the sidewalk

Family is a rewritten text
Fleeting connections that never live under one roof

Here one person's floor is another person's roof
I hear my neighbor having sex but we're not friends
I analyze his bathroom gurgles singing teapot like text
I use my vibrator muffling the sound with a blanket
Sometimes we don't even say hi on the sidewalk
That's just how it is in the city

My view of the city is a valley of roofs
Warmed by people on the sidewalk who are my friends
Where pleasure comes from giving a blanket writing poems from the
survival that becomes my text

Skills Center

Pink drink rings on the white table. Suzy talks about waking up in shelter. Suzy, with long nails, dyed hair, shaved arms, and heavy stubble, telling about the monitor who wakes up the women with, "It's time to get up, ladies," and this includes Suzy, who sleeps on the women's floor. And candy wrappers. Mrs. D comes in then goes out, will she come back, returns with bags of caramels to share. Mrs. D who has been in shelters so long she remembers when the Skills Center was a shelter. Mrs. D makes sure we all get some sweetness. And me and Brad lead the class, excited about our new topic, the To Do Lists of the Homeless, saying *talk about a tough day. People say the homeless are lazy, sit around all day. Is it true? Do you wait in lines? Make a timeline of your day. What's it like waking up in the shelter each morning?* Ben Donaldson, who comes in each week 30 minutes after we've started, looks like he's going to be punished for coming late to poetry class. Ben says when we ask him to make a timeline, *my sense of time isn't the greatest.* Mrs. D is thankful for the wake up call she gets in the morning, frowning she says with the sun in her face and for Mrs. D to spend more than one night in the same shelter means stability and she's feeling good and provided for and like she's on her way to bettering herself and I'll be damned if I want them to write about how tough it is.

Dante's Coup d'État

Ben Donaldson walks into the room 30 minutes after the class has started, his tail between his 60-year-old legs. He's cowering, apologetically ducking some imaginary blow. "Greetings all, salutations. So sorry to be late. Good to be here, though. Lovely, lovely," he says, finding a seat at a far table and sifting through his bag for his glasses.

"Nice to see you, Ben. It's just good that you're here. We're almost done with the freewrites, then we'll read them in a second," I say.

"He should come on time if he wants to be here," Mrs. D shoots her words at me, then glares murderously at Ben. "He's always getting special attention, singling himself out!"

I jump in, "Each of us gets help where we need it and have our own ways of doing things. Now who's ready to read their freewrite... Wally?"

Wally sits with his briefcase in his lap, his arms wrapped tightly around it. "I'm just here to observe. I won't be writing this week. I got a lot of stuff going down. Just got a place at the Sanctuary today. Maybe next week," he says tersely, the anger in his voice just barely masking his terror. "You have no idea what I've gone through the last few days. At least tomorrow I won't have to panhandle. I've got a lot going on and need to finish updating my resumé."

"I'll read my piece," says Mrs. Black. "But first I want to know about the hassles. I know there are going to be hassles. What are the hassles going to be?"

"What do you mean by hassles?" I ask.

"Someone stole my poetry," Mrs. Black raises her voice; a slight tremor is beginning to invade her upperclass British diction. "My poems are being published in this book, and they're crediting my work to a dead woman. To a dead woman. That's why I want to know up front what the hassles are going to be."

"Who are they crediting your work to?" I ask.

"Virginia Woolf," answers Mrs. Black.

Dante, in full fatigues including the hat, has been nodding off up to this point and wakes up upon hearing Mrs. Black's exclamation.

"Hey, my name is Dante. Dante Juan Martinez and I was born in San Francisco in the same projects as O.J. and I'm a veteran. I didn't drink today. At least not before creative writing class." Dante's shopping cart is parked outside and can be viewed from the window. "I have had hard times, hard times on the street. Today, this dude on the street on the street today, panhandling, was saying, 'Spare a dime for a black man.' I panhandle, but—"

"Okay, let's focus. Who wants to read their freewrite?" I am the only white person in the room besides Angie. I definitely don't want to talk about race.

"I don't have a problem with blacks. I am black, you know, we gotta stick together—" Dante continues.

"I don't want to hear you saying you black," says Mrs. D, body stiff, spine perfectly erect. Her head, an automatic rifle, swivels until she has Dante in her sights. "You ain't black till you a black woman, a black woman with only your bible and God's grace to see you through."

"Okay, Mrs. D, sorry to interrupt, but let's move on. Let's get back to the writing. The freewriting is just a warm-up. I want to move on to some poems for us to read and imitate," I say.

"I have something to say, Dante here. I, Dante, have something to say."

"Dante," I say, "We talked about you joining the class only if you could participate according to the guidelines we agreed upon."

"Are you trying to silence Dante? Didn't you say this is a place where we come to share our voices? I, Dante, come from the streets and I have something to say."

Wally gets up, grabs his briefcase, and quietly leaves the room.

"Dante, Wally," I start, then change my mind. "Dante, we want to hear. We just have to talk in turn and give everyone a chance to—"

"I am trying to say something!"

"Dante, other people in the class have things to say as well. You are going to have to leave if you can't wait your turn."

"You want me to leave? Is that what you're saying?" Dante collects his things, adjusts his fatigue hat, zips up his knee-length army jacket, and heads for the door.

Angie speaks for the first time that evening and says, "I don't want Dante to leave. I think you hurt Dante's feelings."

Mrs. Black agrees, "I think Dante should stay."

Ben puts in his two cents, "Dante is an important member of the class and contributes significantly to the group."

Caught completely by surprise at the class' support of Dante, I acquiesce, "Okay, Angie, Ben, thanks for your input. Dante, come sit down. Let's read some of the freewrites now."

Dante is already seated again.

Disrupture

Any anthology is finally a gathering of poems rather than poets.[1] My head is an anthology with Mrs. Black's seagulls who whisper poems to her, Matisse's poem about finding her 19-year-old self and O'Hara and Bishop and what about poem titles and phrases, once theirs that become mine? Mrs. Black says her poems have been stolen and the publishers are crediting her work to a dead woman. When asked who is being credited, she replies, Virginia Woolf.

My co-worker says she can't work with the delusional students. This is the homeless population here, who could possibly deal quite well in society if it weren't for that persistent hallucinatory problem, that nagging drug problem, that annoying little mental illness. *Somebody embroidered the doily. Somebody waters the plant, or oils it, maybe.*[2] Mrs. Black says some book stole her poetry. I don't try to reason with her. I tell her, look, you got a choice to make because people may steal your work, but how about creating work and letting it go, putting it out into the universe and suddenly that tense look disappears from her face. She's been repeating, "I just want to know about the hassles, I know there are going to be hassles, what are the hassles going to be?" And she says, yeah, that's what I'm doing, you're right, that's what I am doing. And later she reads what she wrote while she wasn't participating because she can't participate and her writing soars, twisted and brilliant, it flies across the page, flying in the face of everything, flying, it's the ugly seagull squalling the gospel and it makes me want to go home and write. *I want words meat-hooked from the living steer.*[3] I want to lay at your feet all that makes me breathe *which is not going to go wasted on me which is why I'm telling you about it.*[4]

If language be an orgy, then I want to fuck every word, sound, syllable. Every stolen utterance exalted. I want to do each of you, have been inside the moment of your derived, the moment of your spoken, be able to proclaim, I know you. I have used you and you have made me whole. Dangle the orphans in front of the widows so they may consummate each other. Make an honest woman out of me. If I am the lover of words then I can marry myself.

----

[1] J. D. McClatchy. [2] Elizabeth Bishop. [3] Robert Lowell. [4] Frank O'Hara.

If language be a riot then let me loot. I want to set fire to tall buildings, overturn police cars, steal from Costco and yes, I want to do it all in my own neighborhood. Deeply interested in disrupture, I sign my name on the asphalt and walls. I know we are writing on the same sidewalk and riding on the same pen. I keep keying my name in cement all over the Mission but it's never deep enough and later looks like inconsequential scratches, maybe I need a knife, scratches, impact, maybe I need a gun, scratches, disrupture. Maybe I need a pen. Out of my control, the words have a life of their own. I wonder at *the rebelliousness of my own utterances, their refusal of my intentions, their propensity to place themselves in quotation marks against my will*.[5] And I think of Mrs. Black. Riot. Pillage. Plunder. Things taken by force or fraud, what else is new except now it'd be done under the name of, under my name, by any other name, would plunder sound as sweet? Wild or violent disorder, riot, a brilliant display, riot, something very funny, riot, to grow wild in abundance, riot, yes, to grow wild in abundance.

---

[5] M. M. Bakhtin.

Manic D Press Books

Escape from Houdini Mountain. Pleasant Gehman. $13.95
Poetry Slam: the competitve art of performance poetry. Gary Glazner, ed. $15
I Married An Earthling. Alvin Orloff. $13.95
Cottonmouth Kisses. Clint Catalyst. $12.95
Fear of A Black Marker. Keith Knight. $11.95
Red Wine Moan. Jeri Cain Rossi. $11.95
Dirty Money and other stories. Ayn Imperato. $11.95
Sorry We're Close. J. Tarin Towers. $11.95
Po Man's Child: a novel. Marci Blackman. $12.95
The Underground Guide to Los Angeles. Pleasant Gehman, ed. $13.95
The Underground Guide to San Francisco. Jennifer Joseph, ed. $14.95
Flashbacks and Premonitions. Jon Longhi. $11.95
The Forgiveness Parade. Jeffrey McDaniel. $11.95
The Sofa Surfing Handbook. Juliette Torrez, ed. $11.95
Abolishing Christianity and other short pieces. Jonathan Swift. $11.95
Growing Up Free In America. Bruce Jackson. $11.95
Devil Babe's Big Book of Fun! Isabel Samaras. $11.95
Dances With Sheep. Keith Knight. $11.95
Monkey Girl. Beth Lisick. $11.95
Bite Hard. Justin Chin. $11.95
Next Stop: Troubletown. Lloyd Dangle. $10.95
The Hashish Man and other stories. Lord Dunsany. $11.95
Forty Ouncer. Kurt Zapata. $11.95
The Unsinkable Bambi Lake. Bambi Lake with Alvin Orloff. $11.95
Hell Soup: the collected writings of Sparrow 13 LaughingWand. $8.95
Revival: spoken word from Lollapalooza 94. Torrez, et al.,eds. $12.95
The Ghastly Ones & Other Fiendish Frolics. Richard Sala. $9.95
King of the Roadkills. Bucky Sinister. $9.95
Alibi School. Jeffrey McDaniel. $11.95
Signs of Life: channel-surfing through '90s culture. Joseph, ed. $12.95
Beyond Definition. Blackman & Healey, eds. $10.95
Love Like Rage. Wendy-o Matik. $7
The Language of Birds. Kimi Sugioka. $7
The Rise and Fall of Third Leg. Jon Longhi. $9.95
Specimen Tank. Buzz Callaway. $10.95
The Verdict Is In. edited by Kathi Georges & Jennifer Joseph. $9.95
Elegy for the Old Stud. David West. $7
The Back of a Spoon. Jack Hirschman. $7
Baroque Outhouse/Decapitated Head of a Dog. Randolph Nae. $7
Graveyard Golf and other stories. Vampyre Mike Kassel. $7.95
Bricks and Anchors. Jon Longhi. $8
Greatest Hits. edited by Jennifer Joseph. $7
Lizards Again. David Jewell. $7
The Future Isn't What It Used To Be. Jennifer Joseph. $7

Please add $4 to all orders for postage and handling.

Manic D Press • Box 410804 • San Francisco CA 94141 USA
info@manicdpress.com   www.manicdpress.com
Distributed to the trade
in the US & Canada by Publishers Group West
in the UK & Europe by Turnaround Distribution